THE LURE

THE LURE

Still More Stories of Families,
Fishing, and Faith

William J. Vande Kopple

William B. Eerdmans Publishing Company
Grand Rapids, Michigan / Cambridge, U.K.

Published 2012 by

Wm. B. Eerdmans Publishing Co.

2140 Oak Industrial Drive N.E., Grand Rapids, Michigan 49505 /

P.O. Box 163, Cambridge CB3 9PU U.K.

Printed in the United States of America

17 16 15 14 13 12   7 6 5 4 3 2 1

Library of Congress Cataloging-in-Publication Data

Vande Kopple, William J.

   The lure: still more stories of families, fishing, and faith /

   William J. Vande Kopple.

      p.   cm.

   ISBN 978-0-8028-6841-1 (pbk.: alk. paper)

   1. Fishing stories, American. 2. Autobiographical fiction, American.

   3. Michigan — Fiction.   I. Title.

   PS3622.A586L87   2012

   813'.6 — dc23

                         2012004722

www.eerdmans.com

Contents

Preface

It is important to some people — particularly a few of my relatives — that I relate the world of the stories in this collection to the world in which I, not too long ago, stored my boat for the winter, repaired a tip-up, and started to wonder whether local lakes had safe ice on them yet or not.

So let me, borrowing fairly heavily from earlier prefaces, work toward a clear response: The fishing lures mentioned in these tales are real. The people involved in the actions in these stories are real (although I have altered a name or two). And the fishing spots I describe here are real.

In fact, I hope you get a chance someday to visit and fish many of the spots I mention here. If you live in West Michigan, you should be able to catch largemouth bass near the island on Wabasis Lake, raise a musky or two near the gate on Murray Lake, and hook some salmon upstream from the Pine Street Landing on the Muskegon River. For most anglers, finding one of the points at the mouth of Lake Huron's Duck Bay, the point I describe in "Mother Might Know Best," will probably be more of a challenge. And even more challenging than that will be finding the reed-filled shallows of Eagle Lake's Kuenzli Bay, the bay whose name sets off some sparks between my sons and me at the beginning of "The Young Will Renew Their Hope."

But my memory for events that happened in the past — sometimes years in the past — is not perfect. Further, not a single activity in any of these stories is represented from the slant of anyone but me. And I admit what friends sometimes claim about me — that now and then I tend to embellish or exaggerate.

But with all of these stories I never stop seeking to convey the truth. Thus I stress that the elements of the plots of these stories are true to the nature of my relatives and me, to the ways we generally relate to one another and to friends, to the ways in which we interact with the natural world, and to the memories we have carried away from outdoor experiences.

I am grateful to Wanda, Jon and Tiffany, Joel, and Jason as well as to my extended family. So much of what I do, I do for and because of them. They have provided me with nourishing suggestions, questions, and bits of critique. They also are models for me, in part because they tell wonderful tales themselves.

I also am grateful to my colleagues in and the students of the Calvin College English Department. Together they have worked to establish an environment in which contributing positively to contemporary culture is a common and often achieved goal.

Finally, I wish to thank several people at Eerdmans Publishing Company for skilled help with aspects of this book: Bill Eerdmans, Jennifer Hoffman, Andrew Hoogheem, and Willem Mineur.

PART ONE

Dad, Mom, and I

As a Father . . .

"Anything yet?"

"Ha! — not a very good job of sneaking up on me this time, Dad. That crusty plowed snow by the road gave you away."

"I wasn't trying to sneak up on anybody. Just trying not to disturb the peace. I know you like sitting out here on the shoreline and meditating under this old white pine. But I wanted to check if you've had any flags."

"One false alarm just after I got my tip-ups set. Must have been the wind. The minnow went to the bottom and just lay there. So now I wait. What are you doing up so early anyway?"

"Figured somebody should get up and get some wood in the stove. That way the lounge will be warm by the time everybody else comes down for breakfast."

"I would've tried that myself, but I wanted to get these tip-ups in the water as early as I could. Plus my record of getting the draft started once the flue's gone cold is lousy. I try to light the stove, start some sort of back draft, and usually end up filling the lounge with smoke."

"It takes more than a little patience. I had to shave off some really thin slices of tinder and keep feeding the tiniest flame before I felt some draw. But she's going like crazy now. Can you see the chimney from where you are? See? And now you might as well glance out on the ice because I just saw one of your flags fly."

"A flag? Hey, you're right. About time. Hope it's a fish. I'll go and check."

"Think I'll stay here. At least until I know it's not another false alarm."

"I'll let you know what I see. A little mushy underneath out here. Almost there. Whoa! Dad, Dad! Better come out — the reel's spinning like crazy. I've got a fish on for sure. There — set. Yeah, yeah, yeah. That's a fish. Feels pretty good. Gonna come watch me land it?"

"I would, but the flag behind you just flew. Probably I should go check it out."

"Thanks. I'm busy here. It'd be great if you could help. Can you tell yet? Is it a fish? I can't turn my neck around that far."

"Oh, yeah. The reel's spinnin'. Must be a fish. All the line just went out. Time for one of my famous hooksets. There! It's a fish all right."

"I can hardly believe this — two fish on at the same time. And at least mine must be really good — at first I was able to gain some line, but now I can hardly move it."

"We both must have good ones on. I can't move mine an inch. Wait till everybody else gets out here and sees these fish."

"The kids'll go nuts. This'll teach them not to sleep in so late. But I'm still not gaining on this thing. I pull, and it almost seems as if that makes it mad, because it's like it gathers strength and pulls back on me."

"Same thing for me. Over and over. Hold on a second — I've got an idea. I'm going to try something."

"What? What are you thinking? Wait a second — mine's moving again. It's coming in. I think I'm gonna get this baby after all. Yeah, it's getting closer."

"You'll get it now. I think you'll get it."

"Whoa! You're over here? What happened? Did you land yours already?"

"Naw. Lost it. Must have shaken loose. Guess there's only one fish for us this morning."

"Well, if it's any consolation, this one feels pretty big. Not much line out yet. Here she comes. Come on, baby, just a little more. Now let's get your head up. There we go. Head up. Let me get a grip. Ah, look at it! That's a fifteen-pound fish if I've ever seen one. At least that. The last time I got one this big was maybe ten years ago."

"It's a beauty. I'll go see if any of the kids are up. Not every day they get the chance to check out a pike this big."

"Hold on a second, Dad. Did you notice this? This pike's got a second hook in its jaw. And the hook's still attached to about ten feet of line. This is unbelievable. This fish must have been hooked earlier. And it must have snapped the line. I wonder how long it's been swimming around with this trailer line. That's just plain amazing. As much as pike like thick cover, you'd think this line would've gotten caught in something — some logs, some weeds, some old pilings or something."

"That's the kind of stuff I've always heard pike like to hide in."

"I know. I just don't get this. Catching this fish has got to be some kind of miracle."

"I guess you could call it that."

Keeping the Sabbath

"**H**oly — !" I was suddenly aware of my own breathing.
"What?" Jason had just made a long cast off the
back of the boat.

"Did you see that? Did you see any of it?"

"No — I just heard a big splash, like a bowling ball dropped
into the water. What was it?"

"Aw, I wish you had seen some of it."

We knew a big musky — probably at least a four-footer —
was active in eighteen or twenty feet of water in the northwest
corner of Murray Lake. We knew that since we had fished
through the area three times earlier in the day, and the fish had
followed one or the other of our lures each time, swimming
high, pushing a bulge of water before it, but then turning away
sharply as it neared the boat. Probably it had caught sight of us
or our shadows.

But this last time, in early twilight, it had followed my lure
once again — I was working a Weagle very slowly, side to side,
sploosh, pause, sploosh, pause, sploosh (I would irritate that fish
into hitting, I thought) — and then about fifteen feet from the
side of the boat the fish accelerated, flared its gills and opened

its mouth so wide I could have tossed a football into it, engulfed my lure, apparently discovered that my Weagle was not some dying fish or wounded frog or wayward duckling, shot out of the water in a near-perfect ellipse, all the while shaking its head hard enough to dislodge my lure and send it flying back with so much force that it almost planted a couple of hooks in my forearm.

"Like I said, I wish you could have seen at least some of it. That was about as violent as anything I've ever experienced in nature."

"Yeah, sorry I missed it. I thought I saw a shape behind my own lure, and I was focused out behind the boat at five o'clock. It's getting pretty late now, but maybe you can come back tomorrow and try for that beast again. It might still be active if it never felt a hook."

"I don't think I ever really got a hook into it. Tomorrow? Maybe I could. What day is it today, anyway?"

"It's Sunday. You could try for it again tomorrow, couldn't you?"

"Sunday? This is just plain unbelievable."

Through most of my life, Sunday was easily the worst day of the week. This was mainly because of my mother's unwavering beliefs about how Sunday should be observed. She had grown up in a Netherlands Reformed congregation. After she married my dad, she left that church and became Christian Reformed, but as I have often noted, her childhood church never entirely left her.

When I was a kid, my mother had in place all kinds of rules

about Sunday. As a family we would invariably go to church twice every Sunday — we would have gone more often if our church had offered more services. This was true even when we were on vacation, and my mom would end up picking out churches for us to attend not on the basis of anything she knew about any given church or its denomination but on the basis of whether the building looked kept up and the grounds properly maintained — the way true Christians should attend to things. The only exception to this twice-every-Sunday rule that I ever remember from my childhood was when we camped at Ludington State Park on Labor Day vacations with at least two dozen other families from our church and we substituted a campground hymn-sing for a Sunday-evening church service. It took a year or two for my mother to agree to this, but one year our minister camped with our group and let it be known he would attend the Sunday-evening hymn-sing. Plus, one of my brothers told my mom that if we boys and our sister sang really loudly, which we never otherwise did, we could say that we were witnessing — wouldn't "Kumbaya" do the trick? — to the other vacationers in the Beechwood Campground.

We had special clothes for Sunday. For church in the morning and night, we wore our very best outfits, suits and ties for my brothers and me, her very best dress for my sister. These were our "Sunday clothes." For the time between services we had to wear "good clothes," clothes not quite as dressy as our church clothes, but not play clothes. We certainly were never allowed to wear t-shirts and shorts — for my mom those brought to mind play and recreation, maybe even frivolity, and these most assuredly had no place on the Sabbath.

My mother's rules put a premium on staying inside. It was

best, my siblings and I often heard, if we stayed inside and read something that would be uplifting to us (I actually got away with reading practically the whole Tom Swift series by hiding those books behind a large church-history book). We were never to turn the television on, although we all suspected that my dad would have welcomed our turning it on so that he could check out the golf tournament. And if we did go outside, we weren't supposed to get involved in any games. We could sit, or sit and read. And we could take quiet walks. But we were not allowed to veer over toward Polaski's field, where a baseball game was almost certain to be going on. Nor did we even dare to think about starting up a game of homerun derby with a wiffleball in the backyard. And on vacation, we could walk along beaches and the shores of lakes, but we were not allowed to go out in boats or even to think about fishing or skiing or tubing. The point was, I guess, that we could do things that would help us maintain our focus on God, not on ourselves, and anything that brought pleasure into our lives was sure to lead us to think only or mainly of ourselves.

All these rules became so deeply ingrained in me that even as a college student, on the Sunday of a camping trip with three buddies to the wilds of the U.P.'s Sylvania Tract, I felt compelled with my cousin, the son of my mother's sister, to leave camp and paddle a canoe six miles to our car, drive ten miles to Watersmeet to a church of about twenty people who acted mainly afraid of us, fight to stay awake in the warm and moldy-smelling air of the church building, drive ten miles back to the Tract, and then paddle six miles back to camp. I will never forget how it felt to walk up the path from the shore to our camp-site, sweaty and sunburned and agitated, and then to see Duzzer and the King sitting quietly around a neat fire, the smoke curling tranquilly up between lightly rustling aspen leaves.

For most of the Sundays of my youth, it was the stress of trying to cope with my mom's stultifying rules about Sabbath observance, I believe, that brought on severe headaches, the kind that leave you lying in a dark room, moist washcloth on your forehead, wondering if it was better to live or to die, praying that no one was going to make loud noises nearby or come in and turn on the light.

It was always clear to me that I would have to do a lot of searching to find someone who loved the Lord more than my mom did. I would have to search just as hard to find someone who was more willing to drop everything and help those in need. And I would admit that to live your life with my mother's kinds of rules does have certain advantages. It must be admirable to live with such an attempted focus on God. Plus you have clarity about all moral matters; everything is either black or white. You don't have to wrestle with crippling doubts and waste your strength wondering what to do and what to avoid. And you don't have to be restless; you can accept things and live with simple trust.

The older I got, though, the more clearly I saw that my mother's firm, even fierce adherence to the rule of law was related to a very grim view of life. For example, people from her childhood church did not buy life insurance. And their argument against it made a kind of sense; after all, if you truly trusted God, you would not need to worry about life insurance since God would be sure to provide for you in the face of emergencies.

But it was hard for me to bring the logic of that argument to bear against the fact that my mom's dad had died when I was a toddler and had left my grandma with very few tangible resources. Near the end of her life she had to go to work at the lunch counter of the Woolworth's downtown and would serve my brother and me chocolate sundaes after we had gone to stamp-collecting club at the city museum. I had a hard time getting used to seeing my grandma at that age wearing a greasy apron, complaining about being exhausted from working so many hours, and having to endure rude comments from callous customers.

My dad used to tell about the times he and my mom would visit her childhood church and observe the Lord's Supper. "Observe" as in "watch." He wasn't joking, he assured us, when he said that only about eight people from that church, eight white-haired men, were confident enough about their own salvation to stand up, walk to the front, and partake. In my tumultuous teenage years, I used to think it would be far better to live life without ever once thinking about God and eternity than to live it every day with uncertainty about the state of your eternal soul.

And my mother had some pretty grim sayings to pass on to my brothers, sister, and me. If we would take a trip to the Upper Peninsula and see advertisements for boat rides out on Lake Superior to view the Pictured Rocks, she would notice our imploring looks and say no. Why? Was it because we couldn't afford it? Perhaps some of the time. But most of the time it was because, "If you do everything now, what will be left for you to do later?" I think I can speak for my brothers and sister when I say that doing everything at too young an age was not our main concern; we thought we hardly ever got to do anything.

Another saying had even deeper effects on me. When my brothers and I would wrestle and laugh and horse around, laughing until we would often get the hiccups or cough and spit up a little, my mother would warn us, in a voice so memorably steely: "Laughing now, crying in a minute!" Sometimes she shortened it: "You'll be crying!" I never had a chance to ask why she thought crying had to inevitably follow laughing. But to this day, when I am in the middle of sheer joy — for example, when a healthy son was born and my wife Wanda was holding him and smiling beatifically — I catch myself, ease up on the rejoicing, and worry that as surely as I can think the thought, the joy will not last. And when it occurs to me that generally I'm doing well, that the life I'm living is actually a really good life, I try to change the mental subject because I know that otherwise a small but insistent voice will invariably say to me, "Don't fool yourself. Things are going to change. For the worse. In ways worse than you might be able to imagine. You just don't know about it yet." And hearing that voice makes me try not to take time to reflect on my life in the first place; doing so just leads down toward some level of depression.

I often wonder how my life would have been different if, at the time when I was filling out my view of meaning in the universe from people I loved and trusted, I had often heard something like, "Laughing now, laughing harder in a minute." Do people ever tell their kids stuff like that? If so, what are their family lives like? That time of my life is long over; I will never know the answers to such questions.

You can probably guess that I, now sixty-plus years old, have decided to ignore many of my mom's rules about Sunday when it comes to my life and the life of my immediate family. But it took me a long time, probably longer than you would believe — forty years or so. I almost invariably attend church on Sunday mornings. But I now often use Sunday afternoons and evenings for long walks in the woods, for drives in the country with Wanda, and even for fishing. In short, I use those hours for serenity, for joy, for exploration, for adventure, for play. After so many years, I couldn't take any more headaches.

And my mom, too, certainly had forces acting on her to get her to soften her views on Sabbath observance. One of my brothers and his wife joined a church that did not have regular services on Sunday night. In place of that, many of the members of that church gathered in small groups, "household groups" they called them, and worked to know and support one another. The other of my brothers joined a church that didn't even have those household groups on Sunday night; they met for worship in the morning, and that was that. Further, that brother's daughter Erika got married to a Roman Catholic young man in a Roman Catholic church. Everyone in the extended family went to the wedding, thinking it was a one-time-in-and-then-out affair, an affair that we hoped would not involve too many smells and bells. But later Erika decided to get confirmed and join her husband in that church, which meant in part that they would often attend Mass on Saturday evening and then forget about church on Sunday. And sometimes, we heard, just because Saturdays could get so busy, they skipped the service on Saturday night. Finally, as I grew older it became increasingly apparent to me that my dad never enjoyed attending churches while we were on vacation, churches where he knew no one and where all they sang was one campfire song after another. I'm sure he told my mom how he felt, at least when none of us kids was around. Overall, though, as far as I ever knew, despite all these pressures on her, my mom never wavered in her beliefs about the Sabbath or changed them. She thought of herself as staunch; most of us saw her as stubborn.

Last August, largely at my sister Barb's urging, my extended clan agreed not to go in several different directions for summer vacation but to get as many of us together as possible for a family reunion — up at Les Cheneaux Landing, on Snows Channel near Cedarville, in the Upper Peninsula. This was a place where some in the extended family had vacationed once or more in the past.

As I noted, Barb had instigated this trip, and it was no secret that she did so mainly because she was intent on having Brian's and her two young sons, both fairly recently adopted from Russia, have the same kinds of family adventures that their cousins, now about twenty years older than the adoptees, had had when they were young. Barb's plan was fine with the rest of us, because of the chance it offered for more of the rather crazy adventures we had always enjoyed over the years. And it seemed particularly fine with my mom and dad because it extended the years of their being grandpa and grandma to young and loving kids far beyond the time most elderly couples get.

I made all the arrangements with the Landing, and the more I called up my own memories of the place, the more I thought it would be a great place for those two little boys to have some serious fun with their relatives. The place had a huge grassy area for games of football and wiffleball. It had a beach volleyball court. It had a horseshoe pit (though the boys were probably not strong enough yet for horseshoes). It had a roped-off swimming area with a pure sand bottom. It had a huge dock, extending past an attached boathouse out into the channel for thirty yards before branching to the south for about ten more yards. And it was on some of the most beautiful and productive fishing water in Michigan, cerulean water leading through channels and past islands and into bays and around shoals and connecting, finally, with the main body of Lake Huron.

After we all had arrived and unpacked on Saturday afternoon, most of the older cousins and the adults wanted to sit on the beach and unwind after the longish drive. But Zach and Scott, the two young ones, wanted to see everything and try everything out. They were like dragonflies buzz-flitting about — out on the dock, then to the volleyball court for a few erratic serves, then into their cottage for some cookies, then to the horseshoe pit to toss a shoe only about halfway home, then into the boathouse to climb around inside the boat that Brian had rented, then back for some more cookies, then down to the beach, where they didn't follow their mother's instructions carefully and waded out far enough to get their shorts wet.

"This should be great," I told Barb and Brian. "No end of things for the boys to do. And we've just gotten here. We haven't even gotten on the water yet, and being out there's the best part."

"It sure looks like all kinds of good stuff to do," Barb agreed.

I was worried, though, about the next day, a Sunday. Barb and I and our brothers had talked earlier and had agreed to go with my mom and dad to the one church we knew about in the area, the little white church on the main road between Hessel and Cedarville. We knew no members in the church, nor anything about its worship or its theology. But it clearly was a church, a Sunday was a Sunday, and we had all agreed it was not a good time to make a fuss.

It turned out that no fuss was necessary. We Vande Kopples were all a little uncomfortable when the minister asked us to stand and introduce ourselves after we had assumed the service itself had started. But it was a Methodist church, and we had all heard of Methodist churches. And how could a sermon that included several emphatic repetitions of "God is love" go wrong?

After church, since it was warm and not too windy, we also decided to push a few picnic tables together and have Sunday dinner outside together. After that, in the early afternoon, Zach and Scott started their buzz-flitting again. They were occupied on the dock for a while — using pebbles to try to bomb the little perch hiding among the anchoring cedars. They fiddled around inside their rented boat in the boathouse; they found places for their tackle boxes in the stern and had their rods lined up against the gunnels. Then they tried knocking the volleyball around again but gave that up when they could not persuade any cousin or other adult to join them — too strenuous so soon after lunch, the older ones said, moving only their chairs, and that only to follow the shade.

And then what I had worried about happened. They trotted over to Barb, each winding himself around one of her arms, and asked, "Mom, can we go out in the boat now? Please? We waited and waited, just like you said, so can't we go fishing now? Uncle Bill said it's great fishing territory up here."

Barb glanced at Mom. So did everyone else, just not all at once.

Apparently sensing some hesitation, the boys moved on to their dad and tried to climb onto his lap. "Dad, can't you take us out? We've got all our stuff packed in the boat already. And we won't whine about having to wear life jackets. We promise. C'mon, Dad. Can we go out now? Please. What's that rented boat for, anyways?"

Brian glanced at Mom. So did everyone else, again not all at once.

Then they tried something I viewed as on the edge of risky: "Grandma, don't you want to go out fishing with us? Mom told us you hooked a huge fish up here, the biggest fish anyone in the family has ever had on. Please, Grandma, please, come out in the boat and help us fish. It'll be great. We saw your fishing equipment on your porch. We'll get it for you if you want."

I decided it was time for a walk: "Down to the end of the peninsula and back, I think," I broke in. "And maybe along that angling road toward Cedarville. Never been that way on foot. I'll be back in an hour or so."

When I got back, it took me only a few seconds to realize that Barb, Brian, and Mom were no longer sitting with the rest of my relatives in the shade.

"Where'd those three go?" I asked my dad. "They decide it was time for a nap?"

"Naw. They took Zach and Scott out fishing," my dad nodded out toward the channel. "Took off right after you left."

"You're kidding. No? Well, what do you know — the world

has turned upside down. Didn't think I'd live to see the day. Can you believe this?"

"Having a little trouble, but what can I say? Those little guys were pretty persuasive. You know how once they get started they don't stop. They keep on and on. So all five of them loaded up the boat and headed out south in the channel."

"But how did they know where to go? Barb and Brian have never been up here before. And Mom's been here only a couple times."

"Yeah, but remember that you've taken Mom out on a few boat rides. And when you do that, remember, you can't help talking about where you've caught fish — I don't know how you remember all those details. Plus you've even taken her out fishing a few times. I remember her stories about that one time you took her out with Jason and Matt — all the rockin' and rollin' and noise and commotion. Then she came back and hooked that monster musky right off the dock. Anyway, she said she'd probably show them one of those points you fished with her out by Duck Bay. I'm sure that's where they're anchored with bobbers surrounding their boat. She loves still fishing."

"Well, remind me not to drop down right here and have a heart attack. I think I've already taken my blood pressure meds for the day. Hope they work. Should probably try to take my mind off those five out there. How about some horseshoes until they get back?"

"Sure. I've been hoping for a game, but I didn't want to get one started with those little guys running around where they might get clunked in the head."

"Okay. Why don't you round up the shoes, and I'll ask a

couple of my boys to join us. Probably it's time for the old guys to give the young ones a lesson in humility."

"I'm sure they could use it."

Later, just when Dad and I were on the verge of some serious education of Joel and Jason, Brian's rented boat came around the island and headed for the boathouse.

"Think I'll go help them tie up," I told my playing partners. "Anybody want to help?"

"They know how to tie a boat up," Joel and Jason agreed.

"I think I'll just wait up here to find out what happened," Dad added.

"Okay, by myself then." As I approached the boathouse, those little boys started shouting at me: "Uncle Bill, you should have seen it! It was great! That was the best fishing ever! It was awesome!"

"Really?" I called back as I stepped up on the dock. "The best fishing ever? That's going to take quite a lot, because we've had some mighty good fishing in this family. I'm not sure you could top each and every one of those times." By that time I was on the finger dock in the boathouse and was reaching for their bow rope.

"Oh, yes, we can," Zach stood up and did a little victory dance, plenty of sass in his voice and gyrating hips. "We caught so many fish. We could hardly keep up with them. It was the best time ever." And then both of them turned to Grandma, gave her their biggest hugs, the nearly choking kind, and ran words together: "Thanks, Grandma, thanks. We love you, we love you, we love you. No one else can find fish like you. You're the best grandma ever. Plus you're the best fisherman in the family. That was awesome! Let's go again tomorrow, okay?

Maybe get up early and fish all day long!" And then they were off, clambering up on the dock and along the planks and scooting up toward Grandpa, Joel, and Jason.

"You really got into some fish?" I wasn't sure how much to believe the fairly new members of our family.

"We did," Brian responded. "Mom directed us out to that spot I guess you all call Jackpot Point, and we thought we might find perch or pike, but we didn't. Instead, we found bullheads. Bullhead after bullhead after bullhead. They seemed to be schooled up there feeding on mayfly larvae — and on our worms. We were so busy helping Zach and Scott bait hooks and unhook the bullheads it was crazy. Look at my hands — I tried to be careful but I still got stuck by those dumb barbs a bunch of times. It'll take me the rest of the week to heal up from this."

"Probably true," Barb put in. "My hands are messed up, too, but the boys will never forget this afternoon — that's for sure. You should have heard them cackling and hooting and hollering."

I reached down to grab my mom's rod and then help her step up from the seat of the boat to the dock. When she was on my level, I turned to her and asked, just loudly enough for her to hear, "A little fishing today, huh? And great fishing at that."

"Now, don't you start. Just don't start."

"Don't you think I have some right to start? Maybe years and years of rights?"

"None at all. I don't want to hear it. I'm eighty-four years old. How was I to know that after all those years something would come along and make me start seeing some things in shades of gray?"

Time Is Tapping on My Forehead

I t was my brother Bruce who gave me the idea.

Shortly after Wanda and I woke up that late August morning, we had the same thought at almost the same instant: We decided to put off the work we had to do to prepare for the upcoming fall semester, take the day off, and go for a drive somewhere. As it turned out, we drove north, for more than two hours, all the way to Interlochen State Park, where we knew Bruce and Judy were set up for their last week of summer camping.

As the four of us relaxed around the fire after roasting brats for supper, I started, once more, to wish aloud for something I feared was never going to happen: "Wouldn't you think that just once before he's too old, Dad would agree to come along with the boys and me on our annual Canadian fishing trip?"

Bruce immediately took Dad's side: "All the way around the top of Superior to Eagle Lake? How many hours do you guys spend on the road anyway? About twenty?"

"More like eighteen, unless we run into lots of construction."

"Spending that much time on the road is just about incredible. Tell most people they have to ride in a van that long and they'd probably say their joints couldn't handle it."

"But so much of the drive," my tone rose, "especially south of Wawa and over by Nipigon, is spectacular. Every so often the road runs through rock cuts so deep you feel like you're traveling in a tunnel. When you emerge and glance inland, in some places you see ponds and bogs that surprise you if no moose are feeding in them. In other places you catch glimpses of whitewater gouging its way through gorges. And if you glance toward the lake, you can see stretches of sand beach, then rocky outcroppings, and then, away from shore, channel after channel glistening between islands. I'm not sure where else in the world you could find so many gorgeous and varied vistas that close to one another."

"Still," Bruce was coaxing the fire along with twigs, "you'd be asking Dad to spend almost a full day riding in a van. Two days if you count there and back again."

"Sure, sure, but he'd be spending that time with me and three of his grandsons. And probably Duzzer. Plus, remember that in between those drives we'd have several generations together at a great fishing camp for almost a week. I keep thinking that Dad and the boys would have such richer memories of one another than they get just from spending a few holidays together each year. Man, can you imagine the card games late at night?"

"That's all true," Bruce agreed. "But you know perfectly well that ever since his heart attack Dad's never been very comfortable going anywhere where there's no good hospital close by. Even when they visited us up here earlier this week, he was no more out of the truck and back from the bathroom than he was saying, 'Remind me, Bruce, where the hospital in Traverse City is. I was a pretty sure I knew where it was, but as we came up to the guard-house here I realized I was thinking about the one in Petoskey.' Sometimes he acts as if he's going to have to drive himself to the hospital to be treated for his own second heart attack."

"I know, I know. With me he doesn't always come right out and talk about a hospital, but for years now I've known it's almost always on his mind. But what he just doesn't seem to realize is that when we're at the camp on Eagle, we're only a mile from the Trans-Canada Highway, maybe even less than that, and it's only about twenty-five miles down that highway to Dryden, which is big enough to have a good hospital. I guess I could understand it if he feels uncomfortable about flying to some lake for a day, but we don't have to go on a fly-in — we could stay on Eagle or drive to what the guides call 'action lakes.'"

Judy had been paying close attention: "You also know, right, that Dad and Mom really don't like to do all that much apart from each other anymore? He golfs with the guys once a week, and she has her bowling league, but other than that, they do practically everything together. If one goes out and isn't back to the condo by suppertime, the other starts to fret."

"I've noticed that, too. I don't really understand it, though. What's the big deal about one week of separation? When you've been married for over sixty years, do you have to spend practically every minute together? I just think he doesn't realize how much he'd love getting out in a boat with me and a grandson or two on some great water."

"You know," Bruce seemed to be trying not to sound apologetic, "you should just ask him to go with you to some lake around Grand Rapids. And don't say you're going to stay out all day; make it a trip for just a few hours in the afternoon. He'd probably do that. You probably couldn't fit all the boys in the boat with you, but take one this time, another the next. Or if they're busy — "

"Don't forget that last week we moved Jon to Minnesota to get ready for his teaching job. Plus Joel and Jason have started two-a-days for soccer."

"Yeah, okay, so just you and Dad go. It's not Canada, but at least you'd have him in the boat with you. It's a start. Later you can add one or more of the boys."

"You know, that's not the worst idea you've ever come up with. I guess even little brothers can stumble onto things once in a while. If he'd go out with me around Grand Rapids, that would be something. Start here and move to lakes up north later. Then find some time when a couple of the boys are free. I'm going to call him tomorrow already."

As it turned out, I wasn't able to call him the next day. It took me a couple of days of wrangling with my schedule before I felt I could mark off an upcoming afternoon for one last fishing trip before classes started. But the afternoon I was thinking of was the afternoon of a Wednesday — the day when my dad usually played golf.

"So, Dad," I had reached him on his cell phone, "I've got a modest proposal for you."

"You do? Good. Better than an immodest one. And I can always say no, right?"

"Right — you can say no if you want to. But here it is: How about a little fishing with me next Wednesday? I was thinking we could go out just for the afternoon; I could have you home in time for supper. And we wouldn't go very far — Wabasis has some good fish in it, and it's only about twenty-five minutes from your place. Especially if we go up the back way, out Knapp to Honey Creek and then north. And you wouldn't even have to bring anything. With all the equipment the boys and I have bought in the past few years, I'll have plenty along for both of us. I could pick you up right after lunch. It's a Wednesday, and I know that's usually your golf day, but Wednesday is really the only day that works for me — I've pushed and pulled on my schedule every which way. I know Wabasis pretty well, so I think I can keep the skunk out of the box. So what do you think? Dad? You still there? Dad? Want to go?" I swallowed.

"Huh? Oh, sorry — I was just checking the calendar. Okay, let me be sure about the details. Next Wednesday, right? In the afternoon? Yeah, I think that will work. Sure. I'd like to go. But are you positive you want to go head to head in a contest with me? I don't do things halfway, you know."

"Absolutely. You're sure you won't mind giving up a day of golf with the guys?"

"I always like to golf. But I've been golfing with that group almost every week for the past three months. Great weather for golf this spring and summer — hardly ever got rained out. And it's been a while since I've been fishing with you, right?"

"Yeah, a while. This'll be great. You're positive you want to go?"

"Sure. You going to pick me up, or shall I drive over to your place? I could meet you at the lake, too."

"I'll pick you up — it's practically on the way. I'll swing by a little after noon."

"Okay, I'll get my wrist and forearm loosened up."

Since that Wednesday was after the start of classes in several school districts around Grand Rapids, I didn't expect the launch site to be busy, and it wasn't — we were able to swing around and back right up to the ramp, take our time loading our gear in the boat, and then launch it. I used the trolling motor to take us away from the ramp and along the north shore.

"We might as well not waste any time cruising around the lake. The boys and I have fished our way along this shore a couple of times this summer, and we've had pretty good luck casting Senkos up toward the lily pads. And we've caught pike with spinnerbaits along the drop-off."

"Senkos?"

"Yeah. It's a cool bait — a piece of molded plastic that looks like a small pencil, only rounded off at both ends. You can hook it in the middle and fish it like a wacky worm. Or I like to rig it up Texas style, toss it out, let it start to sink, and then give it little twitches. Often when I lift my rod tip I feel some resistance and I know it's time to set the hook. Here. I'll rig one up for you. I'll put a black one on your line — the bass have been slamming them this summer. I've got the point of the hook just under the surface of the Senko, so you'll be able to pull it through pretty heavy weed cover, but when it's time to set the hook, you'll have to put some muscle into it to drive it home."

"Muscle's no problem. You going to use the same thing?"

"Same bait but a different color — a white one. We'll try to figure out which color they're hitting today and then both use that."

"So I can't quite remember — when was the last time we fished together? Do you remember?"

"The last time? It could have been that time when the boys were little and you went with us up to Les Cheneaux. That was quite a few years ago. The boys and I would troll for pike up and down the west side of Snows Channel, and you usually hauled a lawn chair out onto the resort's dock. You'd toss out a sucker or shiner under a bobber and wait for the pike to notice it, bragging to us before we left the dock that you'd outfish the four of us all by yourself. I mainly remember how when we'd come trolling around that island directly across from you, the boys would make such a commotion, jumping around and waving their arms to get your attention across the channel, that they would almost fall in."

"Ah, yes, I do remember that. I still have an image of them across from me in the channel. It seemed like they were doing jumping jacks in the boat."

"Hold on a second, though — I might have a couple of seasons mixed up. That might not have been the last time we fished together. I think the very last time was the winter after that, when everybody was up at the bio station visiting Bob and Meredy around Christmas. I put out a tip-up for myself each day, and then spent a good part of each day sitting in the station's shanty. And I remember that each morning you and all the grandsons wanted me to auger holes for tip-ups for you too, but if you guys didn't have a flag in twenty minutes or so, you'd all leave me in the shanty and straggle back to shore and into the dorm lounge and start some board game or other. Each time that happened, I told you I'd have to pull your tip-ups if no one was going to attend them — every once in a while a C.O. would stop in at the station — but you and the boys insisted that I leave your tip-ups set up. Every fifteen minutes or so, you promised, one of you would come out on the dorm deck with binoculars and check if a flag was up."

"No one could call us stupid. Why sit out on the ice when you can fish in comfort? Play a little Yahtzee, toss logs on the fire, eat some popcorn, drink some hot chocolate — you never knew what you were missing. Plus it was so much fun if our designated spotter happened to see a flag. Then we'd all race to the door, half kill ourselves flying down the dorm's steps, yank on coats and hats as we went, and race to be the first one across the ice to see if the flag was a false alarm or not. That is, we'd race as long as you minded your own tip-up and left ours alone."

"You know I never poached on any of your action. Once in a while I saw one of your flags fly and timed how long it would take you all to notice. But I've learned not to comment on other people's fishing tactics. Or on how much success they're likely to have if they ignore flags flying for seven or eight minutes. I'm pretty sure that Christmas trip was the last time we fished together."

"You're probably right. But — "

"Oh, wait a second! Dad, Dad, take up the slack in your line! I think you've got a fish on!"

"How could I? I haven't felt a thing."

"There's no way you could feel it — you've got a big loop of slack line on the surface next to the boat. But look where the line disappears into the water. You cast up by those lilies, and now your line is leading off back toward the boat launch. You've got a fish on, and it's swimming away. Reel up and set the hook! Come on, set it!"

"Okay. Here we go. Whoa, would you look at that!" A bass about ten inches long shot from the surface, gave its head a sharp shake, and sent Dad's hook and now-torn Senko sailing back in our direction while the fish flopped back into the lake and disappeared.

"I can't believe it. All that time and I never felt a thing. Did I do something wrong? How do you keep a fish from getting away?"

"Sometimes there's nothing you can do. But you've got to keep your line tight. And sometimes it helps to drop your rod tip to the surface, even below the surface, when they're about to jump so that you keep them from shaking their heads around so much. Sometimes that even keeps them from going airborne. I just think you never got a good hookset on that one."

"Okay. Let's get me set up again. I'm not going to lose another fish today."

"I'm sure you won't. But that was a pretty small fish. I think we'll move first. The boys say I spend too much time fishing shallow water. When I'm with them, all I hear about is fishing deeper, where the big fish are. I think we'll fire up the big engine and head over to the island. The water there drops off fast to twenty feet or more. We'll switch to tubes and fish them down along the drop."

"I'm game. Do you have enough tubes for both of us?"

"No problem. I've got about a dozen blue ones. Why don't you sit across from me here when I run the big motor? That'll help us plane out faster."

When we reached the island, I rigged us both up, and we tried a new tactic. Each of us tossed out a tube, let it settle, and bounced it down the drop-off. Then Dad caught me slightly off guard: "You know, I never had the chance to ask you what it was like to move Jon to Minnesota. That wasn't that long ago, was it?"

"Just a week or two back."

"Well, I've been wondering how it went. When did you leave Grand Rapids? How long did you stay with him? How tough was it to leave him behind?"

"We left Grand Rapids on a Thursday morning. And we thought it was important to stay with him through Sunday morning and go to one of the churches that support his school. Overall that was a good idea. Quite a few people talked to him, and he even met some of the people he's going to teach with. But it started to get really tough for me already in church. They had a congregational reading of a version of the Ten Commandments, and part of that had to do with holding the family in high esteem and honoring father and mother. I didn't need to be reading that right then. Wanda wondered why I stopped speaking right in the middle of a sentence."

"I can see that. I'd be having a tough time too. Did you leave right after church, then? You had more than a little driving to get back home, didn't you?"

"About ten hours' worth. We wanted to do it in one day. And on the way back we ran into thousands of cars returning to Chicago from Wisconsin — I hadn't thought of that beforehand. Still, we didn't leave right after church. Jon wanted to find a Sam's Club for a calling card so that he could call his girlfriend in Honduras. And then we had a last dinner together. Arby's. I couldn't finish my fries."

"So finally you had to say good-bye and drive away."

"Yeah, it was time. That was tougher than I ever thought it

could be. On all of us. I was trying and trying not to tear up, because I knew that would affect Jon, and I don't think I ever let too many tears show on my face, but all that fluid started draining through my nose and making a mess on my mustache. Fortunately, right about then, Jon's landlord drove up and forced us into one quick hug and a few final words."

"And then you just drove off?"

"Yeah. But as we headed across Wisconsin, some tough memories of Jon kept ambushing me: How he as a boy would give me a look that was almost tender in its furtiveness as he would check my gaze to learn if I was seeing the leopard frog he was pointing to in the reeds at Myers Lake. How when he was really young he would always want to sing "Beautiful Savior" before going to bed, pronouncing the vowels in "Beautiful" so precisely, holding "my crown" for a beat or two after I had let off. How brave he was when toward the end of first grade all the parents visited his classroom on family night and he was asked to put on some huge purple sunglass frames and read the story he had composed about going through a secret door in our upstairs closet — we had read some C. S. Lewis to him — and stepping into dinosaur-land, where he befriended Tracie the triceratops."

"At least you could ride along with him and be there to help him move. Remember when you left home for grad school? I was so frustrated, lying up in our bedroom after my heart attack and listening to you, Mom, and Bob going in and out loading up all your stuff — that squeaky screen door! I was glad enough that I had survived and could come home from the hospital. But I would have given a lot to be able to help you pack the truck and then to find that dorm and help get you settled. I had to lie there all day waiting for Mom and Bob to get back home and to hear about the kind of place you were living in. And once they did get home, their report didn't make Woodlawn and Hyde Park sound too safe. Plus they took back a Chicago paper that had a story about finding a murder victim under the Illinois Central overpass a couple of blocks from your dorm. 'What have we let Bill go off and do?' I kept asking myself. Hope I never have to feel that low again."

"I have dozens of memories of that day that I'd like to stamp out. I had to come up to your bedroom and say good-bye to you while you were flat on your back. And yellow. I wasn't at all sure that you were going to make it till I could come home for a visit. I remember that you kept insisting that I take a Vitamin E pill every day. 'They'll keep your heart strong,' you kept repeating. And my memories of getting out on the road and actually moving in are not a lot better. I remember driving the pickup while Mom and Bob kept handing the map back and forth, trying to figure out which way to go. I tried to be patient: 'Well, which is it? Should I take the Skyway or stay on 80?' I remember parking in an alley between gray garbage bins and then loading my stuff onto an elevator that stopped a foot below the level of my floor. That was the only time in my life when I thought of accidents in an elevator. I remember having to humor Mom. After we had moved all my books and clothes into my room, she insisted on having a picnic in Jackson Park, just the three of us, complete with a tablecloth spread on the ground and party napkins that said 'Oh, the places you'll go!' on them. I remember watching as the two of them drove away through Jackson Park, Mom's tight smile framed in the passenger-side window until they passed behind a huge willow. And I especially remember going back to my room, thinking that I should cry, and deciding that the best place to do so would be outside, and then wandering around outside the Museum of Science and Industry discovering that I wasn't able to full-out cry but could make only some constricted choking noises. I felt as abandoned as I've ever felt in my life. But I was also eager for Mom and Bob to get back home so I would know you were all right."

And then he swept his rod above his head, a look of fierce determination in his eyes.

"That was a bite if I ever felt one!" he yelled out. "I've got one, I'm sure of it, and it feels pretty good."

I looked to his rod tip. He was right — it was throbbing irregularly, the sure sign of a fish, not a mass of weeds.

"Keep the pressure on him." I reeled up as fast as I could and moved over next to him.

"I will. I will. I set the hook so hard on this one it probably went through both jaws. Wait a minute. Oh, no, I don't feel him fighting anymore! He's not moving, but my line's not loose. It's like it's stuck. Feels like a big snag. Where could that fish have gone? You think I lost this one too?"

"Just hold on a second. Maybe you didn't lose him. He might have buried himself in some weeds. That's an old trick. Here, I'm going to move us with the trolling motor so that you can pull on that fish from the backside of those weeds. Keep the line tight, but don't yank on it. Just keep it tight. We'll surprise this fish from the back. Here we go. Almost there. Now you've got a different angle on him. Can you get him out?"

"He's loose! He's swimming right up toward us. Ah, there he is. I saw a flash of silver. And a big tail. He's a good one. A lot bigger than that earlier one."

"Watch it, watch it!" I put the net partially in the water, and I leaned over the side, peering anxiously. "He's going under the boat. Smart old boy. He's going to try to cut your line on a keel. Stick your rod tip down into the water. Hurry! Make sure he can't scrape your line against the bottom of the boat. That's it! That's it! But don't let him get up by the trolling motor either. How'd this fish learn all these tricks? There — I've got the trolling motor up. At least that's out of your way. Keep him away from the big motor now, and you're going to get him. Yeah, yeah, yeah. Lead him this way. I'll get him. I've got the net ready. Just get his head up if you can. I can feel it — we're going to get this big dog!"

And then that bass came out of the water hard within a couple of feet of the side of the boat, its head shaking and throwing off jumbled strings of water. I didn't even think, my arms just slid the net over, directly under the fish, and I caught my breath as it fell and settled deep into the cords.

"All right! That's the way. We got 'im, we got 'im!" My dad paused to catch his breath and glanced around to see who might have been watching the fight. I reached into the net for the fish.

"Twenty-two inches, maybe a little more," I gloated. "It's the fish of the summer — at least it's the bass of the summer. I bet it's a five-pounder. Not too many get an awful lot bigger than that around here. Not that I've seen."

"That was great! But wasn't your net job a little risky? Do you always try to net fish while they're flying around in the air? I'm not sure that fish was really tired out."

"You're probably right — he's pretty lively yet. And if he had landed against the rim of the net, I probably would have lost him. But I had the net right there, half in the water, and when he went airborne, all I had to do was slide it over, lift it a bit, and wait. Anyway, the truth is that my arms just acted on their own. It's not like I thought about it a lot. Here, hold him like this, and I'll take a couple of pictures. Now let's get one horizontal. Mom's not going to believe this."

"I bet you're right. Speaking of Mom, what time is it? She said we were going to eat around 5:30. Is it getting close?"

"It's a little after four. We probably could fish for a while yet, but there's no sense in playing chicken with the clock. I'll head back to the launch. It takes a little while to get everything packed up. And we're probably not going to top that fish, anyway."

"Sounds good. I promised her I wouldn't be late."

When we got back to the launch site, we found it no busier than when we had arrived, so I didn't have to wait in any line. We managed to get the boat level on the trailer on the first try and haul it out of the water to a parking spot where we could load our gear back in the van. As I was double-checking the chains and safety strap in the front of the trailer, Dad came up on the other side of the hitch.

"Want to hook the lights back up?" I asked. "I usually unplug them when I launch to make sure nothing shorts out when the trailer gets into the water."

"Sure. Where are the wires from the van?"

"Just to the left there. I tucked them under the tarp. Yeah, there you go."

"Okay." He took the plug at the end of the wires from the car in one hand and the socket at the end of the wires from the trailer in the other. The whole apparatus, plug and socket together, was not very complicated. The plug was a flat four, with three male parts and one female. The socket was a corresponding flat four, with three female parts and one male. And in all my experience I cannot remember anything mechanical that my dad has not been able to understand, operate, fix, and often even improve on. But just as I thought he would insert the plug into the socket, he hesitated, holding the socket steady and turning the plug in his hand. Then he held the plug steady and turned the socket one way, then the other, then the first way again. It was at that point that his eyes came up to mine. I saw an expression of bewilderment, of bewilderment on the edge of panic, and I reached down and took the two ends from him: "I've got it, Dad. It's kind of a funny connection. This is how it goes. Just a little different from the way you had it. We're all set to go now."

And as I turned away to get into the van, I murmured to myself, "Oh, my God, did I wait too long?"

PART TWO

Solo

Justice Rolling Down

If anyone ever deserved a little break, I thought as I drove to the Muskegon River after school that Friday afternoon in October, I was the one. In the past week, I had faced more work than I had thought three skilled and motivated people, working feverishly, could ever complete. But I had somehow managed to finish everything up on my own. The effort, though, had left me so tense that the muscles along the back of my neck felt braided.

At breakfast, Wanda had reminded me that it was time that night for her and her memory-book club to have their annual chick-flick festival. So I was on my own, and when I can do as I wish, I usually choose to fish. Since the king salmon run was near its peak, I had packed my waders and salmon gear in the van before I had left for school.

As I cleared the heaviest traffic on my way north, the muscles in my neck gradually loosened as I realized that the weather was perfect for salmon fishing — it was cool, it was overcast, it was misty. By the time I got to the landing area on the river, I had relaxed enough to feel a little drowsy. But the scene in the parking lot was jarring: vehicles were jammed everywhere, even on the path to the outhouse. "How unfair would that be," I thought, "if I couldn't even find a place to park?" But eventually I did find a legal parking spot and decided to put on my gear and hope for some casting room on the water.

Once in the water, I looked upriver to the overhanging cedar that was doomed someday to be undercut completely and swept away by the current. I gave a little victory whoop when I saw that no one was fishing the gravel bed that extended out from the exposed roots of that tree.

I hurriedly pushed upstream. In the river in front of the cedar, a narrow ledge of what looked like limestone extended downstream on an angle and then back upstream, forming an irregular but noticeable V. Within this V was a large bed of perfect spawning gravel. Below the V was a pool darkened by thousands of zebra mussels on its bottom, a pool where salmon could rest out of the heaviest current. Best of all, over time the rock at the base of the V had been eroded into a gap, and this gap formed a natural gateway from the resting pool to the spawning bed.

Whenever I had fished this spot in the past, it had been easy to hook salmon. I would cast from one or the other side above the gateway, let my fly drift down into the gap, and prepare to set the hook. It didn't even matter whether the salmon were actively feeding. Once they were positioned in or just below the gateway, they were so intent on what awaited them up on the gravel that they would snap at my fly just to get it out of the way.

That late afternoon I had so much fun fighting salmon that I stayed longer than necessary to sort out three silvery fish to take home. In fact, by the time I turned downstream, it was past dusk. Since I had forgotten to pack my headlamp, I moved back downstream taking baby steps, and my dark-water shuffle kept me from pitching over any submerged rocks and let me savor the wonders of the trip.

In such a mood, once I had left the landing, I decided I shouldn't just head back to the freeway and blast my way home. I turned onto a slower road south, a county highway skirting scrubby cornfields, set-back homesteads, and dark woodlots.

A few miles down this road, I tuned into Blue Lake Public Radio. "Next," the announcer said, "we'll hear the Houston Symphony Orchestra and Chorus performing Mozart's *Ave Verum Corpus*."

As the music intensified, my throat constricted, and my nose started to run. I had started to weep. Not loud, chest-wracking weeping, but the quiet weeping that comes from serenity that has surprised. As the sopranos surged, I pulled up to a stop sign.

I have been back to that intersection in the daylight, so I know what was there that night. To my right was a hedge of bushes about five feet high. The trunks and thicker branches of these bushes were black with bark. But the smaller branches were crimson. Behind these bushes and to the side was a pole with a powerful security light.

What I saw as I glanced to my right that misty evening was backlit silver-sheathed red and black tendrils branching and extending boldly against the void. Before pulling away, I rested my forehead on the steering wheel. "My God, my God," I murmured; "it is almost more than I can take in. What did I do to deserve this?"

Add this image to what was already in my mind — the motifs from Mozart and the memories of fighting beautiful and powerful fish — and the rest of the drive home was mainly reverie.

Just as I signaled my right turn onto our street, though, I was startled. A short man wearing a green hooded sweatshirt, having left the sidewalk to my far left, was crossing the street on an angle toward me. As I went into the turn, in fact, he was only six or eight feet off my door. But I completed the turn, gave a snort of slight exasperation, and dismissed him.

I pulled into our driveway, got out of the van, opened the garage door, got back into the van, pulled into the garage, turned off the car, and then grabbed some gear to carry into the house. As I bumped the door open with my elbow, stepped down, and pivoted, I almost stepped right into the man who had been crossing the street. He was standing in the shadows between the van and some bicycles and was aiming an automatic pistol directly at my chest.

Suddenly I was taking my pulse with no hands. And I can remember feeling three emotions at the same time: frustration, because my plans for the rest of the night were shot; anger, because I had been careless enough not to check my rearview mirror as I came down the street; and terror, because I had no control whatsoever over the situation I found myself in. Plus, the hole on the end of the pistol was bigger than I ever imagined it could be.

"Shut up! Shut up! Don't try anything stupid! Do exactly what I say!"

I hadn't said a thing, so it frightened me that he was so jittery. I thought of drugs. The sooner I can give him whatever money I have, I thought, the better. I wasn't sure how much money I had.

But he didn't ask for money: "Keep that hole in your face shut, and listen. Get back into the driver's seat and reach across and open the passenger door."

I turned and climbed back into my still-warm seat, opened the passenger door, and wondered if Wanda was home and, if so, what she was doing. When he got around to the other side of the car, he surprised me: He didn't climb into the passenger seat but reached through the open door and opened the sliding door to the rear of the van. Then he started to climb into the back.

But the three salmon I had caught were lying on a newspaper on the floor right next to the door — I had taken one of the rear seats out. "What the . . . !" he said as he swept the fish back under the rear seats. "Now I'm going to stink like a fish."

I hoped that I had left some hooks lying near the salmon. *Sit down hard on a treble hook and see how you like it* — I could at least think boldly.

"Don't turn! Don't look at me!" He banged the pistol on the back of the seat in front of him. "Okay, you mother. We're goin' for a ride."

It was then that I knew I could no longer do what he said. I was almost lightheaded imagining all the things he might have in mind for me, and every one of them was costly, kinky, or deadly. Then the little knowledge I had of similar situations, my trace of training, kicked in.

A couple of years earlier I had heard a story about our former provost driving downtown with his wife. When they came to a stop sign, a man jumped into the back seat and told them to drive on. Gordon thought otherwise: "Mary, get out right now!" he shouted, and both of them jumped from the car and hustled away. Gordon took the car keys with him. Apparently, the man fussed for a while under the steering wheel but then climbed out and vanished into an alley.

"Get it together," I thought. "If there's any flash of speed in you, use it now." I silently slid the key out of the ignition. I drew a deep breath. Then I threw open the door, bolted toward our house, lunged against the side door with my shoulder, caught my foot on the rug on the landing, regained my balance, turned around, slammed the door, locked it, turned off all the lights in the kitchen, yelled for Wanda to douse the lights around her and get down, and called 911.

But I was panting too hard to put words together. And I was afraid that the guy, in vengeful fury now, would start shooting through windows. So it took me a few minutes, huddled under the kitchen table, to explain simple things such as what my name was, where I lived, and why I was calling.

Two policemen arrived in less than three minutes. They came in fast and quiet, no lights. Out of their cars, they advanced on the garage. As soon as they were certain that the guy had fled, they knocked on our side door and beckoned me outside. We stood in the front yard, and one whose name badge said Simon asked the questions.

"What did he look like?"

"He was really short — about five foot two or three. I don't think he expected someone six foot five to get out of the van. If he hadn't had that gun, I would have tried something, and I think he sensed that. I have rakes and a spud leaning against the garage wall."

"Skin color?"

"Not sure, but pretty dark."

"African American?"

"I think more like Hispanic."

"How about his hair?"

"Couldn't really tell — he was wearing a hoodie."

"Anything else distinctive? Glasses?"

"Yeah, I think he was wearing glasses. Why can't I remember better? Did I tell 911 he was wearing glasses? I think I told them he was wearing glasses."

"You were out of your van when he confronted you?"

"Yeah, I turned and took a step or two, almost right into him."

"And then he forced you back into the car?"

"Yeah."

"That's kidnapping then. What all did he say when he was in the car?"

"He was, like, 'come on, you mother, we're goin' for a ride.'"

"And that's when you ran?"

Just then another squad car pulled up, this one with K-9 on its side. An officer wearing a bulletproof vest stepped out and released from the back seat a German shepherd straining against a thick leather leash.

"Where?" that officer asked Simon.

"The garage."

The dog didn't even have to enter the garage and smell the van. He sniffed around on the driveway leading to the garage, ran to the fence on the west side of the backyard, waited for the officer to lift him over the fence and climb over himself, and then ran off down the street to the woods along Plaster Creek. The officer who hadn't been interviewing me ran after them as backup. Simon trotted to the squad car and yelled that he was going to follow them, keeping tabs on their location via radio.

After they had left, I stayed outside; I was afraid that if I went in the house, I wouldn't be able to make myself come back out. I sat on the front porch and tried to remember what the neighborhood used to look like.

After about twenty minutes, the officers and dog all came back in Simon's cruiser. Simon walked over to me on the porch.

"It was weird," he shrugged. "They had a strong scent for a while, and then it went across Union Street and just disappeared. Sorry. He might have had a car parked there, or he might have jumped some other driver."

I was surprised how strongly I was coming to believe that things would be close to right again if they could just catch the guy.

"Remember anything else while we were away?"

"No. I guess I'm not trained for stuff like this."

"Well, if anything comes back to you, here's my card. And we'll let you know if anything develops overnight. You going to be okay?"

"I hope so." I didn't say that I was sure the guy would be coming back after me.

Wanda had already been in her pajamas when I came crashing into the house, so she had stayed inside when I had gone back out. From my 911 call, she knew most of what had happened, but I had to fill her in on some details. I knew I would have to wait until daylight to go back to the garage and get my gear. I also knew that those three beautiful salmon were going to start to break down since I wasn't going to have the nerve and energy to retrieve them and filet them that night. Wasting them was its own kind of crime.

After I had taken a long shower, and while we were lying in bed, Wanda asked if I thought I would be able to sleep.

"Well, most of the adrenaline has worn off. I'm not quite as jumpy. But some stuff sure is knocking around in my head."

"What stuff?"

"Well, all my life I've heard about God's sovereignty, his control, not a hair shall fall — all that. So the past several days look like a big set-up — wear me down, bring me way back up, and then slice my guts out."

"I don't know for sure about all the theology. Who does? Maybe God allows some chance in the world. Or maybe being sovereign means that once he allowed the possibility of sin in the world, he had to allow all of its possible evil effects to play themselves out. Or maybe he has some deep design with pain that we won't know about until we see him. But I do know all this: You had a chance to wade a river and do what you love, you really got into some fish, we didn't lose a single possession, you could have been shot but weren't, this probably messed with your head but everyone we know will be eager to help you get over that, and now your head is on a pillow next to mine. Plus any guy desperate enough to chase someone into his garage is sure to do some more risky stuff soon and get caught. If you didn't have angels watching over you, I wouldn't know who did."

I didn't have the strength to argue. Without having faced what I had faced, I thought, she couldn't really know the truth.

But in every detail that I was ever able to check on in this world, it turned out that she was right.

Longing

*A*t *last*, I said to myself as I snugged up the safety belt on my waders and scanned the rapids of the St. Mary's River just west of the Canadian Sault, *I will see if the pink salmon fishing here is anywhere close to as good as I've been told.*

I had heard such extravagant stories about fall fishing for salmon in this rapids that I suspected I had been set up: No place, I thought — particularly no place within a couple of miles of two sprawling mills, one steel and one pulp — could hold that many fish, could attract scores of anglers, and could still leave all of them feeling as if they were exploring one of the world's wild places.

My introduction to salmon in the St. Mary's had come several years earlier, during a stormy afternoon of a late-August family vacation. We had camped at several parks along the south coast of Lake Superior and were ending our trip with a brief stay at Brimley State Park. On that Friday afternoon, the wind was driving cold rain in so hard off Whitefish Bay that it felt like sleet. In such weather, Wanda and I decided, trying to take the kids hiking, even if we could find a somewhat protected trail near Monacle Lake, would probably leave us with three little boys huddled under cedars whimpering through blue lips that the next time we went on vacation, we should leave them back in Grand Rapids with their cousins.

So instead we took them to the Michigan Sault, where we thought they would love checking out tankers in the locks but where they were more interested in watching people slice slabs of fudge and in rummaging through bins of "Indian" moccasins made in Taiwan. Before we left the city to return to Brimley, I drove down along the river, past the Tower of History and the museum ship, and started to turn around in a small park south of the power plant.

And I would have just turned around in the parking lot if I hadn't noticed that forty or fifty people were casting lures from behind the railing along the river and that every few seconds one of them would snap a rod up and back in a decisive hook-set.

"Something's happening here," I said to Wanda; "I've got to check it out."

"You always do. But we're not going out in this. And you'd better leave the car running with the heat turned on."

I parked, stepped out and struggled into my rain jacket, and then ran over to the railing, fighting to keep the hood over my head. When I got to the railing and looked down into the water, I saw the dark backs of scores of two- to three-pound fish cruising along and then wheeling away from the wall in large subsurface clouds.

"What are they?" I yelled to the guy to my right.

"Pinks!" he shouted back.

"Pinks?" I moved closer to him.

"Yeah, pink salmon; they're in here pretty early this year — we've had a bunch of cold nights in a row."

I've got to try for those, I thought, and fought the wind back to the car.

"The river's full of pink salmon," I reported, "and people are catching them by the bucketfuls, just by casting little red or green spoons. Anybody want to give it a try?"

"I do, I do, I do," chirped our three sopranos in the back.

"Hold on a second," Wanda gave me a sharp look. "You're not going to stay out in this weather, are you? And no way are you taking these little guys out there. We're not coming home with boys who can't start school because they've caught pneumonia on vacation."

So I started to simmer a bit but agreed to drive away, trying not to stare at the images in the rearview mirror as several people set hooks and then held throbbing rods high in the air and other people scrambled to pick up long-handled nets.

That night back at Brimley, I ran into a park ranger and told him about all the wild action I had seen.

"I don't think I've ever seen so many people fighting fish at the same time," I said. "It looked like a DVD I have of river fishing in Alaska."

"Where were you exactly?"

"At that park south of the power plant. Alford Park, I think the sign said."

"Ah, man, you got just a little taste. You've got to go over to the Canadian side and fish the rapids. One minute you can see patterns on the rock slabs under several feet of water, and the next minute the pinks swarm in and the water goes dark. It's like fishing on the world's fifth day. You can catch fish until you can hardly reel."

"I'm dying to try it," I responded, "but our vacation's all but over — we leave for home first thing tomorrow."

"Well, maybe some other time."

That night I promised myself to find a couple of days in some late August or September to make the five-hour trip from Grand Rapids to the Sault to fish the rapids. But year after year, finding that time seemed nearly impossible. For one thing, it was difficult to preserve white space in my daily planner. For another, whenever I started mentioning specific days to Wanda, she would start quizzing me about the wisdom of such a trip.

"All the way up to the Sault for a few hours in a river you don't really know? What about all the rivers closer to home? Doesn't the Rogue have a good run in the fall? Or the Muskegon? We've driven up around Croton Dam on color tours and have always seen people catching salmon. And how far away is the Pere Marquette, anyway? Why drive past several great rivers chasing some dream?"

"Well, I know it might be a little wacky, but it is a dream, and you know what happens to a dream deferred."

"This is not Poetry 101. We're talking about family time and finances."

"I know. I know. But I hear that when the pinks run up the St. Mary's, they're so thick they actually change the color of the river."

"Well, if you've got it stuck in your head that you absolutely have to go, you'd better take a couple of days just before classes start and try to work this out of your system."

And so, several years after our brief visit in the rainstorm, I was finally able to head back to the U.P. I left home late one

Thursday afternoon, drove to the Michigan Sault and got a hotel room, and started to arrange gear for an early start the next day.

The next morning, as I crossed the international bridge into Ontario, everything and everyone seemed in place to stoke my sense of expectancy. From high on the bridge I could see dozens of anglers fishing the rapids, but apart from groups of two or three standing at intervals along a long cement berm that ran to the south from the compensating-gate dam, each one seemed to be off in water to himself or herself.

More than enough room for me, I thought.

When the officer at the border asked why I was visiting Canada, I said that I was hoping to find pink salmon in the rapids.

"I don't fish, so I don't know for sure if they're in. But about every fifth car coming through this station the last couple of days has had fishing equipment in it. You can find out about the salmon run at any local sporting goods store. Know where one is?"

"Yeah. I've got an address from a natural resources magazine. Thanks."

I had written down sketchy directions to Western Automotive, a car-parts and bait store, and after a couple of misadventures with one-way streets, I found it and asked about fishing licenses for nonresidents.

"Are the pinks in the river?" I wondered aloud as the clerk was sorting through stacks of forms.

He looked at me quizzically and then shot back: "Where else would they be — at the casino? No, sorry about that — I couldn't resist. They're in the river, that's for sure; the question is how far up the river the huge schools are. We've heard lots of stories about guys tearing them up down in the North Channel. But it's been really cold at night lately, so some of those fish should have moved all the way up to the rapids."

"I can't wait to give it a shot." I paid for the license and hurried out. While paying better attention to the one-way signs, I wound my way to the parking area for the rapids.

After I pulled on my waders and checked that I had everything I needed in my vest, I walked west and came to a lock on a small shipping canal that turned what had been a broad peninsula into an island. As I stood on the edge, I immediately started wondering what lure I should try first. For although the water in the channel went to black in the depths, I could see schools of fish cruising only a few feet below the surface. When I looked around a little more, though, I saw the signs: fishhooks with bold red slashes through them.

Talk about making you wait! I thought as I crossed the canal and started down a dirt path, cobbled here and there with baseball-sized stones. I was so eager to get to the river that the half-mile or so I had to walk seemed like two miles. But just before I thought I'd be passing under the international bridge, the trail curved off to the left and I came through an opening in the bushes and stood gazing out past the berm I had seen from the bridge.

"Where to start?" I wondered. The rapids was as big as some of the lakes I fish, and I could see promising-looking spots all over.

On the inside of the berm were dozens of enormous boulders scattered off in a channel to the south, boulders with hunched-up shoulders of water on their upstream side and crystal-fringed emerald eddies on their downstream side.

I had heard that anglers could probe around carefully on the outside of the berm if not too many of the compensating gates were open, and as far as I could see, only three were letting frothing torrents spill from the level of Lake Superior. There on the outside of the berm were several tongues of water surging through cracks in ledges or through gaps in jumbled lines of rock and then spreading into extensive fans. Also outside the berm were extensive pools of smooth water lying immediately below white water that looked too fast to wade through.

With so many good-looking spots, I decided that I should cover as much water as possible. Farther, I spurred myself on, over there, past that boulder with the brownish veins, maybe on the other side of that rust-colored ledge, or maybe below that, in the water around what looks like a jumble of red and white cobblestones.

As I moved, I saw a few pinks when my shadow sent them flashing away, but I hooked nothing. And I started to wonder what would make a state-park official tell a tourist tales of schools of fish turning crystalline pools dark.

After an hour, I was starting to ache, especially in my lower back, and I felt rushed, almost manic. At one point I decided to tie on a different lure, and as I formed the loops of the knot, I was in such an agitated hurry that my hands were shaking.

You just can't fish such big water this way, I finally told myself. You're moving too fast to notice anything. And you'll wear yourself out. Pick a spot and try to figure it out.

I found a boulder overlooking a large underwater slab of what looked like sandstone with a pool of moss-green water upstream and a mass of sand-colored rocks downstream. Maybe if I'm still, I thought, I'll be able to cast to a fish or two darting from around those rocks and heading across the slab into that deeper water.

When the fish came, they didn't come from downstream. They didn't come one by one. And they didn't dart.

They came from upstream, moving with the current, seven or eight or nine pinks in a shape-shifting cluster, moving calmly, almost regally, veering neither to the left nor the right.

Yes, oh, yes, I've found some fish, I exulted.

But my exultation was premature — in the time it took for the fish to pass over the slab, I was able to make several casts, but not a single fish hit.

It was maddening. I could watch my red-and-gold Little Cleo doing its shimmering dance as the current brought it across in front of the pinks, but not one of them gave even a hint of interest in it.

In my frustration I was reduced to the level of trying to converse with fish: "What's the deal?" I asked. "On Fridays you play hard to get? Or you're on an afternoon break from biting? Or I have to chant something? What?"

Of course, by then the small school had made its stately procession out of range of my casts, and I had to wait for other fish to swim into view. When they did, I tried several of the lures I had carried out to the rapids with me. But the pinks were supremely uninterested.

Finally I learned a critical bit of information by accident. I had switched to a silver spinner, and just after I cast to a few more approaching fish, I shifted my weight and caught the edge of a boot on a notch in the boulder and almost fell off. I did a wrenching little dance to regain my balance, and in doing so, I jerked my rod skyward and that jerk gave the spinner an erratic flash. It was then that a pink turned to nose it without quite taking it in.

"So that's what you want — a little flash!" I exhaled. After that, each time a pink came into range, I tossed the spinner out and gave it a series of sharp twitches. It would flash and flutter, and sometimes a pink would turn and take it in. I ended up landing five or six. And I was singing the one aria I knew all the words to right out loud; the noise from the rapids kept my voice from bothering anyone.

Only when an angler on the berm yelled past me to a guy who had walked out into the rapids wearing a muscle shirt, cut-off jeans, and Converse high-tops did I realize that the light was reflecting off the water in burnished streaks and that I should probably head back to the van and begin the long trip home. So I made my way out of the rapids gingerly and started back along the path.

While I was on the path, my sense of exploration and conquest led me to notice and savor: large stones like enormous anthills breaking through the slate-like surface of the sheltered water of a pond, a miniature red maple with translucent green marsh grasses bowing rhythmically before it, several willow leaves with curled tips caught in an eddy below a riffle in a brook.

These images stayed with me as I pulled off my gear and crossed back into the States. And they stayed with me as I headed down 75 toward home until NPR aired a special program about the challenges of controlling lamprey in the St. Mary's watershed.

As soon as I came through the door back in Grand Rapids, Wanda called from the basement, where she does her memory-book work, "Well, did you catch those fish you've been dreaming about all these years?"

"Yup, you might as well start calling me Izaak. The water up there is almost impossible to wrap your mind around. It's as clear as a spring, with rocks and boulders in fifty or sixty more colors than I have names for. You could probably spend half a year studying just the shades of red. And the good-looking fishing spots lead on and on. For a while, I was exploring more than fishing. But finally I settled down, and I figured out how to get some pinks to bite. Got five or six, and they fought like dervishes. For most of the way home I thought I could still feel them thrashing around on the end of my line. It was well worth the trip."

"Good. No, great. Nothing like working things out of the system. Now maybe you won't feel such a crazy pull to go flying off hours away from home chasing some dream a stranger happened to put in your head."

"I get what you mean, but. . . ."

"But what?"

"It's just that once I found out how to catch those pinks, I didn't really have enough time to do them justice."

"Heaven help us."

You gullible fool! You should have listened to Wanda, I chided myself. I had clumped in waders as fast as I could to the far north end of the berm on the Canadian side of the St. Mary's rapids and was leaning against one of the buttresses of the compensating-gate dam, pressing as much of my backside as possible against the concrete.

It had been about a year since I had explored the rapids and finally figured out how to get some salmon to hit. But Wanda had made it clear that she did not fully approve of my driving five hours to fish when I had the Rogue, the Muskegon, and the Pere Marquette Rivers hours closer to home.

But I was now in a sabbatical semester. Why not pursue a little adventure? And I made what I thought was an especially smart move in asking Jon, who was on a short break from school, whether he'd like to come along on this jaunt to the U. P. Wanda's resistance to such a trip would be sure to lessen if I took a son along.

It turned out that Jon was eager to go, mainly because he had heard that impressive numbers of birds of prey funneled down along the St. Mary's on their fall migration, and he hoped to see some, maybe even a jaeger or two.

So we packed our gear and got an early start, running into some construction for a few miles on 131 around Greenville, but thereafter enjoying mainly clear roads and hardly any highway patrolmen (Michigan was mired in a budget crisis and had cut back in almost every department, including the state police).

When we got to the Sault, things went amazingly well. So that we wouldn't have to drive all the way home after fishing, I reserved a hotel room in the Michigan Sault. The line of vehicles on the international bridge was as short as we had ever seen it, and the Canadian border officer we talked to, once he heard we were heading for the rapids, was brisk and efficient, almost cordial; it turned out that he was an avid angler himself. Without a single wrong turn, I drove to Western Automotive, where we bought licenses and some yarn flies tied in a pattern I hadn't seen before. And finally I drove to the bridge south of the power plant and then across it to the parking lot for the rapids.

As Jon and I sat under the raised rear hatch of the van, both of us pulling on our waders, it began to rain, not hard but steadily, the kind of rain I always think will get the fish going.

Perfect, I thought. *The rain will make it a little harder for us to see into the water, but since it's so dark, the fish should feel freer to roam the rapids, and the low pressure bringing this rain can't do anything but make the fish aggressive.*

Just as I finished that thought, the rain intensified, changing from a pat-gap-pat-gap-gap-pat-pat to a steady thrumming and then to a violent pummeling; once Jon and I had our waders and raincoats on, we stepped out from under the van's hatch and felt assaulted, as if the rain was trying to beat us down.

"Dad," Jon shouted over the pounding, "this isn't worth it. I'm going to take my waders back off and stay in the van for a while. Maybe just read."

"But with your raincoat over your waders, you're as protected from the rain as anybody could be."

"I know, but this is a mess. The rain actually hurts my head and shoulders. And I don't know how you're going to tie any kind of knot in a downpour like this. I'm not sure you could even make a decent cast."

"Okay. No one's asking you to do anything you don't feel like. But I'm going to make the hike and at least give the rapids a shot. Wouldn't seem right to me to drive all the way up here and not use the time I have. I won't stay forever, though; I'll check back with you in an hour or so."

So I grabbed my spinning rod and walked off and crossed the lock. After briefly scanning the several trails heading off to various sections of the rapids, I picked the one I remembered best, the one that led most directly toward the international bridge. I followed the path as it made its traverse of the island to the river, head down, fighting the heavy rain and the intensifying wind, irritated that water blowing off the edges of my hood was spotting my glasses. But eventually I made it to the water's edge. And then I hesitated. I had about thirty yards of the channel inside the berm to cross, but the yellow bull's-eye that I remembered on the side of the berm, the mark that showed what line to take through the rapid water, wasn't visible — either it had washed off since my last visit or the rain was obscuring it.

No choice, I thought; you've got to get over there, and the longer you wait, the scarier it's going to seem. And so I stepped down into the channel: Good gravel at first. Really good traction, some of the best traction ever. Oops — this is getting too deep. Back off. Try more to the north. No, too many underwater boulders. That's trouble — don't want to get an ankle wedged in there. Why do I always forget to take a walking stick? The more arthritic my hip gets, the more I need a stick. Go south. Looks better. This is probably the route I've always taken. Yikes — water's turning darker again. Getting deeper. Two more inches and it's coming over my waders. Veer off again. Still more to the south. Careful. Get a good plant with one foot before you raise the other. Don't get careless. Water's going down. A little less pressure around my middle. Ah, I think I've found it. This is the way. Good gravel again. I've got to remember next time — stay off to the south. The channel's wider here but safer. I reached out and up with my free hand to the top of the berm.

Just as I started to step up on the rocks, pivot, and slide a hip onto the berm, I heard thunder from downstream, probably a mile or two south. Maybe the storm will veer off to the east, I hoped; at least some of the clouds are churning off that way.

But what seemed to be the heart of the storm came straight up the river, and soon I was in a place where I had always told Wanda I was too smart to ever let myself get caught — in the middle of a thunderstorm while sitting in a boat or standing in a river. Lightning was all around me, ambient lightning above, making the greenish-black clouds pulse with pink and white light. Then thick bolts ripping downward, one apparently striking near the Tower of History in the Michigan Sault, several others stabbing the hills out beyond the iron mill on the Canadian side. I couldn't fight off the memory of the description my friend Gary once gave of how one of his high-school buddies was foolish enough to play golf in a thunderstorm, got struck by lightning, and later was found smoking and burned and dead, his glasses fused to his skull.

Think, I measured out my breaths; *clear your head. You can't head back toward the shore. And no way can you get down into the wider and faster main channel outside the berm. Maybe if you stay on the berm and move up under the bridge, you'll be somewhat protected, even though it's hundreds of feet in the sky. Better yet, hustle all the way up next to the dam. That's as much protection as there is out here.*

I was right on the edge of full-body tremors when I finally made it to the buttress of the dam. I noticed that it had a jagged vertical crack in it, a crack unfortunately too narrow to wedge any part of my body into. But I tried. *It takes you a while to learn,* I finished my train of thought, *but it seems as if someone's telling you not to drive so far to fish. So get through this and then don't ever think about coming back.*

Just as I was daring to believe I might survive, a bolt of lightning struck off to my left, maybe two hundred yards back in the scrub on the island, close, terrifyingly close, close enough that I could feel the hair on the back of my neck stand up and rub against the inside of my hood. *Maybe I'm not so safe,* I worried. *What if it hits the dam?* I was sure that the steel in the dam would conduct electricity, but I was hoping desperately that concrete would not. Steel was above and to my sides, but I was leaning against concrete. I just couldn't remember whether concrete conducted or not. I took off my glasses and held them under my raincoat.

As I was trying to remember the last time I had reviewed with Wanda where all of my life insurance papers were, I noticed a chilly lick of air. Then less force in the rain, maybe even some gaps in what had been a torrent, and finally some bright streaks in the clouds boiling toward me from the south. *It's past, mainly; it's past. It shouldn't matter now if Wanda doesn't remember where all those papers are.*

And in fact right then it didn't matter, since more chilly gusts hit me, the really dark clouds once above me had moved off to the northeast, and the water still falling around me, I finally figured out, was not rain from storm clouds but wash from the international bridge.

As even that wash diminished, I was able to see down into the pool below the compensating gate directly to my right. A huge king salmon was cruising regally around that pool, passing only eight or ten feet below my feet, then off toward the next buttress, then up along the foot of the gate itself, then back below my feet again.

It's teasing me, I patted a couple of pockets of my vest to check where I had stored my spinners and flies. *It's just daring me to catch it. If I had a long-handled net, I could almost scoop it up when it goes through this part of its circuit. I've got to hook that fish — no salmon can taunt me like that and get away with it.*

But a quick glance at my watch showed that I had been away from the van for over an hour already, and, with all the thunder and lightning, Jon was almost certainly wondering whether I was safe. I decided that I should hike back and check in with him.

I walked south on the berm, surprised now at how wide it actually was — it had seemed like a tightrope during the storm. And it was easy to find a path through the inside channel back to where the trail I had taken met the water.

On my way back to the van, the trail presented more challenges than it had earlier, one muddy pool after the next, debris floating in all of them. But somehow it seemed shorter this time.

When I reached the edge of the parking lot, my first look toward the van made me think Jon had decided to conk out. In fact, I thought, he must have put his seat down as far as it can go. But when I reached the side of the van, I realized Jon wasn't in it. *Maybe,* I mused, *when the rain finally stopped, he decided to get out and do some birding, either along the roadway here or across the lock on the island.* But when I checked the back of the van, I saw that his waders and raincoat were gone. He must have headed to the river, on a different path than the one I took.

Now here's a fine ke — no, I caught myself, *not a good metaphor for a fishing trip on which I've been to the river and haven't even gotten a line in the water.* But some metaphor like that would be appropriate, since once I got back on the island I would be in a tough situation, literally between a lock and tailrace. I could take the path I had already been on to return to the river, and Jon could take the path he had already been on to return to the van. Or I could take a path south of the one I had already been on to head west, and Jon could take the one I had been on to head east. Or I could pick any one of the paths to get back to the rapids, and Jon could simply bushwhack in the other direction to get back to the van.

It would be wisest, I knew, for me simply to wait by the van until he figured out I was no longer in or around the rapids and came back looking for me. Otherwise, we could be passing each other by on the island for all that was left of the day. But what if Jon had gotten hurt or disoriented? The arguments on the side of waiting were strong, but waiting — at least for me in that situation — was impossible.

So I gathered up my rod once more, crossed the lock, and headed off on the same path I had taken earlier. It was, it seemed to me, the most well traveled, the one that Jon might well be led to eventually. But at no point along it did I catch any glimpse of Jon. For that matter, I caught no glimpse of any living thing other than a couple of mergansers seemingly trying to press themselves into rocks on the edge of a pond.

Fortunately, when I got back to the river and waded out into the inside channel five or six feet so that I could have an unobstructed view to my right and my left, I made out what I thought was Jon's gray raincoat south on the berm, quite a ways south, down near the Volkswagen-size boulders in the inside channel. I used some heavy line to wrap up a corner of my beanie and tie it to the tip of my rod. Then I waved the rod at Jon, rhythmically back and forth, like some enormous metronome with a colorful tip.

Turn, Jon, turn! Don't you see me? Look this way. I was summoning whatever telepathic powers I might have unconsciously developed. At first he seemed to be focused on something below him on the inside of the berm, but then he turned and must have seen me, for he gave a quick pump with his right arm.

Instead of walking along the berm until he was across from me, he sat down on the berm and slid into the inside channel and started to wade back toward the island. I was too impatient to wait for him to make it to the shore and then follow it all the way up to me, so I started to walk down toward him, preferring to stay a few feet in the water so that I could avoid the mucky potholes along the shore.

"Hey," I called as I came up to him, "did you get out here and worry about where I was?"

"I was up and down the berm about as far as I could go in both directions and was starting to think you couldn't be out here anywhere. So I was going to head back to the van."

"Which way did you take across the island, anyway? I never saw you on my way back to the parking lot."

"It would have been hard for anyone to see me. I made my own path and came out south of where we are now, down thataway. I had to fight through some pretty thick stuff."

"It's no wonder we missed each other. I got caught on the berm during all that lightning and ended up pressed against that buttress up there. Never even made a single cast. How about you? Did you just walk the berm looking for me, or did you get some casts in?"

"I thought I saw some fish in that pool over there, just beside that cluster of boulders with the scrubby bushes growing in their middle. So I made a cast and almost immediately felt something, either a take or a snag, but I ended up losing my fly. Can you believe that — one cast and my fly's gone? And then I realized that you had all the extra lures and flies. So I ended up walking along the berm with nothing to cast."

"This has been one messed-up day. Worse, really, than any other day I've ever spent up here, and none of those has ever been great. I guess I'd say we should just head up to my path and take that back to the van. There are a few hours of daylight left, but this place has about done me in. We might as well head back to the hotel, get cleaned up, and then take our time and have a nice dinner. Have you been to Antlers lately? If you can stand all the bells and whistles, the food's pretty good. They've got this huge hamburger."

"That sounds okay to me. I'd love to get into a mess of salmon, but I came along mainly to see some raptors, and not many birds have been flying today."

So we walked side by side up to the terminus of my trail. Just as we stepped out of the river, two guys came around a little bend in the trail toward us. One, who was wearing a St. Croix hat, was about thirty years old, I thought; the other had to be twice that age.

"Do any good?" St. Croix asked.

"Naw." I leaned my rod against a clump of alders. "We've had a lousy day. First I got caught out on the berm in all that lightning. I don't know if you were around here during that storm or not, but I can't remember when I've seen lightning like that. When the worst of the storm passed, I decided I had better head back to the car and touch base with my son Jon here, who had stayed in the car. Good idea to check on him, I guess, except that when I was returning to the car, he was heading toward the river — and on a different trail than I was on. Ships in the night. Just a few minutes ago we finally found each other. And now there's probably still enough time for us to do some fishing, but I've had it up to here with this place. This is not the first time I've driven all the way up here with stories of fantastic fishing echoing in my head and then not done diddly. I guess it's time for us to call it a day. And from now on, I'm going to learn to do my fishing closer to home."

"Where're you guys from, anyway?" St. Croix had sat down on a flattop boulder near the shore and was fitting sandal-like felt-packs over the boots of his waders.

"Grand Rapids. Michigan. The Lower Peninsula. Quite a drive. Five hours up and five hours back."

"I know." St. Croix was back on his feet. "I'm from Troy, over by Detroit. This is my father-in-law. He used to live in Michigan, too, but a few years ago he moved to Pennsylvania. He tries to get back every fall to make a trip up here with me."

"All the way from Pennsylvania to fish here?" That was a little much for me to believe. "Do you guys know some secret spots or something?"

"I might," St. Croix grinned. "I went to Lake State for four years. And one of the main reasons I went there was so that I could fish this rapids. Most every afternoon in the fall and the spring, fifteen minutes after classes got out, I was in my car and on the way over here. There's almost unbelievable fishing in this rapids. You know, you could tag along with us if you wanted. No sense in driving away ticked off. Where we're headed there's more than enough room. And plenty of fish to go around. Isn't that right, Dad?"

His father-in-law chuckled. "I guess you could say that. I've popped about 800 milligrams of ibuprofen just so my joints are ready to fight all those fish. This trip is probably the highlight of my year."

I glanced at Jon, who gave me his it's-fine-with-me-if-you-want-to look. "You really sure you wouldn't mind having us tag along?" I asked. "I'd love to get into fish here the way I've always heard about, but I don't want to hold you back or be in the way or anything."

"Forget about it." St. Croix gestured as if he were wiping crumbs from a table. "We don't move too fast. No way you'd hold us back. But there is a stretch where the rocks have some algae on them. Not a long stretch, but it's so slippery it's worse than ice. How are you guys set for traction?"

"Jon should be good. He's got studded soles. But all I'm working with is ordinary wader soles. Probably not good enough. Thanks for your offer. That was unbelievably kind. But it probably wouldn't be safe for me in these waders."

"Hold on a second." St. Croix unslung his rucksack and unzipped it. "I've got an extra pair of feltpacks right here. They're a little worn, but they still work. You're welcome to use them. Here. Put them on while I tie three-way swivels on my dad's and my rods; then we'll head out."

It took me a minute or two to figure out the clips on the feltpacks, and when I finally finished the job, Jon, St. Croix, and his father-in-law were all waiting, pretending not to watch me. "Finally," I shrugged. "I think I'm ready. Which way across this channel?"

"South here and then straight across." St. Croix stepped into the water, holding his and his father-in-law's rods in his right hand. His father-in-law took his upper left arm, and Jon and I followed close behind them. We made it across the inside channel and climbed up on the berm so quickly that I forgot to make a mental map of our route. Then we turned and, single-file, made our way south along the berm, until we were just above what I, from reading about the rapids, knew was the Canadian hole.

"Here's where we head into the big water." St. Croix turned toward us and grinned. "Make sure each footfall is secure." We stepped from the berm onto pumpkin-size rocks and then into the current of the main channel. He led us just above the edge of the Canadian hole, then he veered right, then straight for a couple of minutes on a slate-like ledge, then left and back to the right around an emerald pool, and then paused. When I looked up and turned to check how far we had come, I felt a shot of adrenaline.

"How far out do you go?" I tried to keep all signs of shock out of my voice.

St. Croix laughed. "Didn't I say where we're headed? Sorry. We usually go all the way across."

"All the way across? The main channel?" I shifted my feet among the rocks. "I didn't think that was possible. I've never seen anyone all the way over there."

"Sometimes it's not possible to go all the way. When they have five or six gates of the dam open, it's not, but today they only have a couple open." St. Croix pointed to the west end of the dam, the end opposite where I had been huddled earlier, where water was boiling under the raised gate and into the rapids. "Today this is a stroll in the park."

"If you say so. I think I'll be better off just concentrating on where I'm putting my feet and not look around anymore. This feels like total exposure. I've never been out in the middle of such big water. Not sure where I could even find another channel this big. What is it — about a quarter mile across?"

"All of that. I know I've never fished any water bigger than this. But we'll be to the other side soon, fifteen minutes tops. Ready?"

His father-in-law took his arm again, and we set off once more, moving cautiously through the rocks, shuffling along ledges, skirting the deeper pools, grateful when we came to stretches of gravel. When we made it to the other side, St. Croix climbed onto the rocky bank, turned right, and led us north for a few minutes. Just before we came up under the international bridge, he stopped. "Here it is," he said with a satisfied smile, "right out in front of us — maybe the best spot on the river. Probably one of the better spots in the world."

That seemed like exaggeration to me, but I was in no position to protest. I had some breath to catch, partially because making it across the whole main channel took more than ordinary effort and partially because I was still feeling the effects of adrenaline after my mid-river realization that I was much farther out in this river than I thought anybody ever went. Plus I wanted to take an angler's look at the spot St. Croix and his father-in-law had traveled so far to fish.

About twenty yards up to my left was one of the enormous concrete supports of the international bridge. Below it, water was spilling from both sides into a frothing whirlpool. The water from the whirlpool released onto a stretch of jagged rocks, some red, some off-white, some a mix of red and off-white. These rocks made me think that a crew of sledge-happy workers had been let loose on a street paved with red and white bricks and had pounded the bricks into fragments and then come up with some way to transport them to the river and scatter them here. Running down the middle of this stretch was a band of deeper-colored water, water that signaled a trough through all the rock fragments. That trough spilled into a pool of even darker water, a pool that looked big enough to swallow a UPS truck. All across that pool I could see fish porpoising.

I moved closer to St. Croix, who had his box of flies out.

"How do you fish it?" I suspected I already knew the answer, but I didn't want to blurt it out and then find out I was wrong.

"Set up a dropper rig," he responded, "and make sure to use a long leader. You can get by with heavier stuff if you've got fluorocarbon. Got any? Fourteen pounds? Good, that will work. The leader has to be at least four feet long. Longer than that would be even better. Two light sinkers are all you'll need — about this size. And I usually find that purple egg-sucking leeches work best. Got any purple?"

"No. I've got some in orange, but no purple. Won't orange work?"

"Not as well. Don't ask me why, but purple is always the best. Here, take a few for you and your son. You're probably gonna need a few. Okay, once you're all rigged up, cast into the trough and let your fly sweep along it and then down over the edge and into the hole. If we watch each other as we cast, we should be fine. The one farthest downstream goes first, then the next one to his left, and so on. Cast straight out in front. Once a few of us hook a fish, the fight will carry us downstream, and the four of us will be pretty spread out. Sometimes you'll hook one in the trough, but most of the time the hit will come just after the fly is swept over the edge into the darker water. Here, I'm all rigged up; I'll show you. This will be fish number-one for the trip."

"A fish on your very first cast?"

"Just watch."

"It's all true what you say about those kings, but there's something about fighting the pinks that really has stuck in my head."

Twilight found the four of us back slogging along the path on the island, and as we walked Jon was having a playful debate with St. Croix's father-in-law. They had been near each other as they had fought and landed several fish, and the good spirit they had developed had lasted.

"Better believe it's all true," the father-in-law almost snorted. "When in the twenty or twenty-five years of your young life have you seen fish that big erupt from the water like that? And thrash on the surface when you get them close. My stars, those kings were like miniature tornadoes. If I had to clean off my glasses once from all their splashing around, I had to clean them off a hundred times."

"I had that too, all that water in my face, but give the pinks credit. What attitudes!" Jon clenched a fist before his chest. "First they have to be stubborn. Once hooked, they could have made it easy on themselves and headed downstream, but no! What do they do? Swim straight up against the current. And whenever I'd get one close, it would go into this wild twisting frenzy on the surface. A couple wrapped themselves right up in my line."

"But still," the father-in-law went on, "just think about over-all power. Did you see that one monster king I had on there toward the end? It jumped once it finally realized it was hooked, and then it just took off. Straight down the river so fast and far it ended up spooling me — and I had at least two hundred feet of line on. Plus I was doing my best to chase that fish. But no way I could slow that thing down. Or catch up to it. That was just brute strength."

Now I had to join in: "But what about that Atlantic I landed, my last fish for the day? Wouldn't you say that an Atlantic, pound for pound, is the most powerful thing in the rapids? I mean, did you see the way it reacted when I set the hook? It ran straight away from me for at least twenty yards, all in about two seconds — I think it just about fried the drag in my reel. And then it was airborne: leap, run, leap, run, leap, leap, leap again, run some more, leap a last time. I couldn't believe its energy. I eventually landed it, but, you know, I almost felt unworthy to catch a fish like that."

"It was a bit of a surprise to find an Atlantic in the rapids this late," St. Croix said as the four of us lined up single file to cross the lock, "but it was a special gift. They're a great fish, and I think it's fantastic that my alma mater has been stocking them the past few years. Once the word gets out a bit more, people will be coming from all over the world to try for them. Well, here we are, back. Dad and I are over on the far side of the parking lot."

"We're right near the entrance," I responded; "we took the spot of what looked to be a couple of college students who were leaving just as we drove up. But thanks, guys; thanks so much. I can't tell you how much I enjoyed that."

"Absolutely," Jon added; "that was fantastic. Talk about saving the day. That was probably the best fishing of my life. Now I can't wait to get out of these waders — I don't think they breathe the way they were advertised. See ya." He headed off toward our van.

I went on: "I don't know if I'll ever dare wade across the whole main channel on my own, but it was great to be able to do it today. I'll have to sit down and think for a while to remember if I've ever had fishing like that before."

"Well," St. Croix said as he extended his hand to me, "it

really was no trouble. And it was a blast to watch all the fights. A couple of times, we had four fish going at the same time. I'm glad you got to experience some of what the rapids has to offer — didn't seem right for you to drive back to G.R. with the wrong impression in your head."

"No room for any bad thoughts now." I unbuckled the safety belt of my waders. "I'll just have to remind myself every once in a while that there are fishing spots like this left in the world."

"Oh, yeah. And there are other great spots not too far from here. Take the Garden River for one."

"The Garden?"

"Yeah. It's down Highway 17 a ways toward Sudbury. It doesn't get the kings that come into the rapids here, but it gets a really heavy run of pinks. I've been there days when I couldn't even plant a foot without almost stepping on two or three fish. You should drive back up here sometime and check it out. The only complication is that most of the Garden is on native land, and you're supposed to fish it with a Band member. So it pays to have a full day to get over there, get paired up with a Band member, and then travel to a spot on the river."

"That sounds great. I'll have to hope for a chance to get back up here sometime."

"You won't regret it."

"Thanks for all your help. That was a great day. Take care now."

"Yeah, maybe we'll run into you up here again, maybe even next fall," St. Croix said, and then he and his father-in-law turned toward their car.

When I joined Jon under the hatch of our van, I turned toward him and kept my voice low: "Could you hear any of what he said to me?"

"Nope. Too far away. What was it?"

"He told me about another spot up here — a river down 17 to the east."

"Can't see how it could match this rapids."

"It's different, I guess. I take it that the water isn't as big, and it doesn't attract as many kings, but it gets a really heavy run of pinks."

"Really?"

"Yeah. I guess you can almost walk across the river on the backs of pink salmon."

"Okay. But there's one thing you'd better remember."

"What's that?"

"You'd better be careful about letting Mom hear you talking like that."

An Angler's Paradise

The nature of eternity is not something I'm comfortable discussing with lots of people, especially fellow Christians, because I'm sure they would say it's something I should never even think about. But ever since I was a little kid, I have been troubled — pretty seriously troubled — by more than one thing I've heard or read about the life in heaven that awaits us after death.

When I was as young as four or five, I sometimes could find no way to get my mind to stop its terrifying knocking-about and let me fall asleep. I would work myself into a cloying sweat and then finally have to clump my way downstairs and ask my dad how he dealt with the issue that was scaring me. And what was that issue? It was the whole matter of eternity having no end.

Although it didn't surprise my dad, hearing this surprises many people, because they seem to relish the idea of life without end. They joyfully sing choruses with words like, "He shall reign forever, and ever, and ev . . . ev . . . er." They talk with no reservations at all about going to one's *eternal* reward or about finding *everlasting* peace and rest.

One man I know misses the teenage daughter he lost in a horrific car accident so much that he actually thinks she occasionally appears to him and talks to him, most commonly shortly after he wakes from a night's sleep. He says she sits at the foot of the bed and whispers to him, telling him not to worry about her. I'm skeptical of such apparitions, but it's clear that he looks forward almost desperately to being with her forever in heaven. Other people I know talk about spouses they lived with and loved for sixty or seventy years — they still carry their scent with them, they say — and how they long to be reunited with them and never have to endure separation again.

But the whole notion of existence without end was scary to me as a child, and it is still probably my greatest fear. I can't toy with it, as I do with some of my fears, bringing them up and then trying to fight with them, all in the hope of conquering them and of growing stronger. No, any time this fear appears as even a small mental throb, I have to force some other thoughts, just about any other thoughts, into its place.

And why don't other people see things my way, I wonder? Just about everything that makes sense to us now makes sense because of an expected ending, a rounding off. Events aren't events without a conclusion. Stories aren't stories without an end. Songs aren't songs without a last line. Who would want to spend ten thousand years, doing no matter what, and then look ahead ten thousand more years and see no conclusion whatso-ever? In general I like being me, but the thought of being me forever, of having no conclusion to the weight of self-awareness, brings on the deepest anxiety. Things just can't go on and on and on. How could I live "ten thousand years, bright shining as the sun," and see no possible end? A million years? How could I always and irrevocably be? And could you even imagine what eternity would be like if you were to spend it in hell? Even as I write these words, I'm on the edge of tremors, and I can feel my pulse throbbing in my neck.

I've also been troubled by what I've been led to believe will be a major activity in heaven. I'm not sure exactly how the thought got settled in my head, but the thought in fact is rooted there deeply: the thought that we'll be doing a lot of standing around singing in a choir. I guess the thought came from so often hearing and singing phrases like "celestial choir," "jubilant chorus," "flaming tongues above," and "no less days to sing God's praise." For some people there is probably no sweeter hope and expectation than to be able to sing with the perfected voices of masses of talented others in heaven. And I like good choral music probably as well as anyone. But I have several deeply negative associations with choirs.

For one thing, when I was in early elementary school, my church started a junior choir, and my parents decided that my brother Bob and I should be in it. In some circumstances that might have been just fine, but in those circumstances we were the only boys in the entire choir. Twenty-two girls and two boys. Some people might be inclined to make a smart remark or two, something like how the odds for us certainly were good. But we were still too young to think or care about odds; girls still had cooties, and to associate at all with them was to put ourselves in danger of becoming infested. Plus we'd be judged sissies by our peers, the other boys.

But our parents forced us to participate, in part, I have always suspected, because my dad helped come up with the idea for the junior choir in the first place. So we went, but we resisted singing. When the director noticed our silence, she would come and stand right behind us, forcing us to make some kind of noise, and we did, but we tried to sing an octave or two below the girls, an effort that for us, in those days before puberty, was clearly impossible.

Similar trials came into my life when I reached junior high school. At that time, the Christian junior high schools in Grand Rapids sponsored what was known as the All-City Boys' Choir, led by Trena Haan, under whose direction, I was told, one should feel honored to sing — people said she was a legend. Now I suppose it was an honor to be chosen for this choir in the first place. And in some circumstances I might have enjoyed the whole experience. It's just that every Tuesday, when it was time to climb into our local music teacher's car for the ride to Grand Rapids Christian High School, I had to do so in plain sight of my friends, who were usually doing things like practicing the shot put or shooting free throws. They didn't think being in any choir was cool. Plus I had to get into that car with four other boys, none of whom ranked very high on our school's tacitly agreed-on classification of stereotypical manliness.

For me, the final knock on choirs came when I was in early adolescence and found that suddenly one Sunday our pastor, whom I admired quite a bit and with whom I was thinking about working toward making profession of faith, no longer was in the pulpit. What had happened? The whispered word around church was that he had abandoned his family, abandoned his church, abandoned his denomination, and probably abandoned his faith. For what? For the arms and charms of our senior choir director; she had seduced the pastor and gotten him to run away with her, everyone said. With the perspective of many additional years, I now realize that I shouldn't have blamed just one of the two people involved in an affair, and I also realize that I shouldn't have associated the shortcomings of one choir director with all choir directors and even all choirs. But I was young then, and I tended to throw blame around somewhat indiscriminately.

Knowing what you now know, it shouldn't surprise you that I have numerous sharply focused conversations with God in which I describe for him what I think heaven should be like. Some friends tell me I should listen more and be more pliant and accepting, but I have always liked many of the Bible stories about Jacob, especially the one about the lengthy wrestling match.

So I have serious talks with God about awareness of time. Wouldn't it be possible to exist in heaven and continuously be, as they say, "in the moment"? That is, could we not exist in heaven and never have the slightest awareness that time was flowing from a future into the present and then fading into the past? Couldn't we enjoy the wonders of an ever-present now? I hear about people who get into what is called "flow," a sense of complete immersion in an activity, like surgeons in the operating room or musicians while they play. After they emerge they say that while in that state they lost all sense of time passing. They were completely focused on what they were doing. That sounds really good to me, in part because I think I have had some similar experiences. I have had moments in which, to an extent, I lost some track of myself as a temporal entity, and that somehow was a pleasant lightening.

Most commonly I have such experiences during moments of excitement and hyper-vigilance while fishing, and thus another thing I wrestle with God about is whether it wouldn't be possible for at least some of us in heaven some of the time to take a break from all the singing and go fishing. As I imagine it, such fishing would be not entirely unlike the fishing we do now on earth, but it would have many wonderfully exceptional aspects as well. Maybe I'm imagining the "new earth" more than I am heaven, but in either case I think I have good ideas for God to consider.

The way I imagine things, the waters we would fish would resemble the waters I admire every time I follow the Trans-Canada Highway around Lake Superior and reach the northwest coast, a bit past Marathon, Ontario. From the bluffs and cliffs along that coast, I see verdant islands set in turquoise waters, islands with horizontal whispers of mist brushing their highlands. These islands are separated from one another by glistening channels, they have rocky spits extending from them in capricious arcs, they have pickup-sized boulders resting imperiously in water off their coasts, and they offer bays on all sides, so that there is always some possible lee. Down from the mainland into the waters cradling these islands flow rivers, one every few miles. These flow from dark pools over small cascades through chattering riffles and into Class 3 or 4 rapids. Follow these rivers upstream and you will generally find mazes of connected shallow lakes, blown-down fir trees all along their shorelines, or large inland seas that drop off quickly from gravel-studded beaches to black and frigid depths. In all these waters swim all kinds of freshwater fish, each kind in its ideal environment. Get on some of these waters in a boat or canoe or kayak, or get into some of these waters in waders, and you will feel a continual sense of beckoning, of being called around another point, into another cove, to the edge of another pool.

Ask many people what they think fishing in heaven might be like, and they say that in heaven they will catch a trophy fish on every cast. I disagree, for more than one reason. For one thing, such fishing, in my experience, poses no lasting challenge and soon becomes boring. I had such fishing for sockeye salmon running thickly in a river in Alaska once, and after sorting through dozens of easily caught fish for my limit of five, I left my fly rod propped against a stump and started poking through alder thickets in hopes of spotting a moose or two. The angling was too easy.

For another thing, I don't believe that fish in heaven will suddenly be transformed into easily fooled creatures. In fact, I believe that each fish will display the deep magic of the essence of its kind, with all of its kind's unique wariness. So heavenly steelhead will know if your fly is traveling at less than the precise speed of the current. Heavenly muskies will veer off and disappear if the start of your figure eight is not smooth and accelerating. Heavenly smallmouth bass will be able to tell immediately if you've allowed reel grease to rub off on your jig and will refuse your offering, no matter how enticingly you present it.

For yet another thing, I believe that heavenly fish will greatly extend their range. Just think of how many of our streams have lost their proper pH levels because of the assault of acid rain. Or think of the streams in which trout can no longer spawn because of the muddy runoff from enormous construction projects. Or think of all the lakes that have been polluted with chemicals used, for example, to cure leather. In heaven, I believe, such waters will be restored, and the fish we love to pursue will be swimming in them once more, giving us the opportunity to angle for them in waters that are unavailable to us in this life. Some of us will, for the first time ever, see what a grayling looks like as it sips down insects on the surface of a pellucid mountain stream.

To have any success, we will in fact have to do something that some people believe will be unnecessary for us in heaven: learn. I understand these skeptics' point — that creatures that are somehow perfected will never need to add a thing to their knowledge again. But throughout my life I have heard so much about developing all of our talents, loving God with our minds, and working with God to cultivate his creation that it's impossible for me to believe that he would have us stop expanding our minds in heaven.

So we will probably have to learn. God will encourage us, because I believe he is a creator who delights in how his creatures can grow and develop. He will, I believe, take joy in the ways we come up with new lures, in the ways we think of to put old lures to new uses, and in the ways we figure out how to catch fish in habitats we have little or no experience fishing in. He will honor our inventiveness, and the appeal of the quest will be expanded.

With fish and fishermen such as I have described, perfect angling will be a possibility. To my way of thinking, this would be angling in which we make every cast with constant expectancy. We won't get a hit on every cast, but hits will come often enough that we never stop believing that one is about to come. We will fish in a state of constant belief and focus. When we catch a fish, we will be so eager to catch another that we will have to remind ourselves to slow our breathing down.

In heaven, everyone will practice catch-and-release fishing.

The especially wonderful thing about this practice is that every fish we release will immediately grow bigger, stronger, and smarter. And after a release, we will never have to wonder what happened to the fish we returned to the water; we will return to our home or to a fishing lodge and be able to call up on a special screen an image of each fish we released earlier and see where it has positioned itself and get an idea of what it is setting itself up to do.

On this same screen we will be able to call up images of the fish we hooked on earth but never got a chance to see. How I would love to see the fish I fought for twenty-five minutes on the dock at Les Cheneaux Landing. It was huge, I know, probably a Great Lakes musky, but I never got a glimpse of even its back; the hook pulled free and the fish never bit again. Another time I was fishing with Duzzer in a fairly shallow bay near Connaught Point on Eagle Lake. I have to admit that I wasn't paying the best attention to my casting and retrieving at that point; Duzzer and I were talking about ways in which our lives since high school had not turned out exactly as we once had thought they would. And that's when my Crane bait just stopped in the water, as if I had run it up against the back side of a boulder. After the stop, though, my line began to move, and I finally realized I had a fish on, one that felt like the biggest fish of my life to that point. "The net, get the net," I hissed at Duzzer; "I'm leading it toward this side of the boat." I could feel the fish shaking its head back and forth powerfully, and then my Crane came free and popped to the surface. When I reeled it in, I noticed that that balsa-wood bait had a sizable chunk missing in its back just behind the eyes. I now have that bait resting on one of the shelves in my office. On the heavenly screen, I would love to see the fish that was able to tear a chunk out of my lure and shake its way off my hooks.

In heaven, when we walk down to the dock through the soft mists of morning, we will make the joyful discovery that waiting in the boat for us are people we should have been able to fish with more often or more properly on earth. One person I would like to share a boat with is my Grandpa Abe.

Before he died, I, about seventeen years old then, would occasionally drive to his house on the west side of Grand Rapids and take him out to Cranberry Lake to try for some bluegills and sunfish. I picked him up and drove him to the lake, but he decided where and how we should fish. And invariably he had me row to a stretch of lily pads in the northeast corner of that lake, where we put baited hooks under bobbers, tossed them as close to the lilies as we could, and then waited. Then we waited some more. His posture seemed to imply that there was no fish alive that could outwait him — keep the bait in the water and sooner or later the fish, having only modest psychological resources, would have to break down and eat it. So he thought. Usually we caught nothing; I spent most of my time sassing back to all the nearby red-winged blackbirds who had apparently decided we were invading their private space.

I asked my dad whether he had ever fished with Grandpa. He said that, yes, he had fished with Grandpa, but that after several days of catching no fish or only one or two, my dad decided to give angling up entirely and switch his attention to golf. No matter how well or how poorly he hit the golf ball, every time he went he was able to have action, action that he could legitimately call golf.

"So why does Grandpa keep on fishing?" I asked.

"It's Hollander stubbornness," my dad replied. "His dad got him started in a boat. But as far as I know, he's never really caught more than a couple of fish per outing, and it irritates him so much that they won't take his bait that he just keeps on going out. He never really switches tactics, and he doesn't often switch locations. He says the fish should take his bait where he puts it — and be grateful for it! It's hard to believe, but he's trying to make sure the fish do not have the last word."

So I would like to take my Grandpa Abe out with me and fish with what I have called "constant expectancy." And I would like him to hook into at least one big fish, one that would thrash wildly on the surface, one that looked so big that both of us would start to feel the adrenaline throbbing in the tips of our ears ("Don't lose him, don't lose him, let the drag do the work and we'll get him!" I would yell), one that would make determined runs under the boat and then back, one that wouldn't stop thrashing around even when it was nestled within the cords of our net. I wish that he could fish because of the pleasures of the best that fishing can be, not because it sets the stage for a long-running and futile battle of wills. That's what I would like.

I'd also like to come down to the dock and discover that my former colleague Ken was waiting for me in a boat. Ken was well known for his love for fishing. Any time the weather was overcast and humid, right on the edge of a storm, his greeting to me was not "Good morning," or "How you doin'?" but, "I bet the fish are snappin' today!" Then he would rapidly tap his thumb against his clumped other fingers as if his hand were the mouth of a big and hungry fish.

By the time I really got to know Ken, however, he had contracted amyloidosis, a disease that he had done nothing to bring on himself and that none of us understood, really. It had something to do with turning healthy muscle tissue into starch or fat, we heard, and we could believe that, because Ken just kept getting weaker and weaker. We imagined that his heart was turning into blubber. He became so weak, he told me, that he couldn't even pull the starter rope on an outboard motor. Rowing a boat was out of the question. "How about getting a powerful trolling motor?" I wondered. He did, but that turned out to be trouble, too, because after a while the battery needed to be recharged, and Ken couldn't even lift that from the floor of his boat to a seat, let alone carry it anywhere.

In his last days, he had to resort to organizing trips with his friends on a walleye charter boat in Lake Erie. All he had to do was get out of the car, negotiate stepping from the dock to the deck of the boat, sit down in a comfortable chair, watch the rest of us as we set lines, wait for a downrigger to go off, and then stand up and take a rod that was handed to him. On one fairly wavy day, I remember kneeling in the stern of the boat and holding fast to Ken's belt, which went around him almost twice, as he reeled in a nice walleye. On the last trip we ever made, even reeling was too much for him.

In heaven I'd like to take Ken musky fishing and watch him heft a nine-foot heavy-action rod with a one-pound bait attached, cast that bait out over the water thirty yards or more, reel it in with vigorous jerks, and then do a crisp figure eight at boatside, toward the end of which a musky over fifty inches long would appear from the side and T-bone his bait and he would fight the thrashing monster long enough for me to put down my rod, get the net ready, and capture the beast. Then Ken could extend his arms and hold up the trophy, which would weigh thirty-five or forty pounds, while I snapped several pictures. He would flash that lopsided grin of his. That's what I would like.

No matter whom we would be with, at some point during each fishing excursion in heaven, we would round a bend in a river or come around a point into a quiet cove, and there would be the Lord himself, beckoning us over for a meal on shore. He would have a fire going, on which would sit a blackened cast-iron skillet with fish fillets, onions, and potatoes in it. Already around the fire would be those we loved most deeply in life, eager to ask how the fishing had been and giving us exuberant slaps on the back and hugs.

No matter what we were fishing for on that particular trip, the Lord would be preparing our favorite fish to eat (I'd like some walleye and whitefish). And he would have heavy loaves of bread ready for us to tear chunks off and chew (I have always been partial to dark rye). If we happened to finish what he had handed us, and wondered if there were seconds or even thirds, we would learn that he never ran out of food. And we wouldn't ask how he managed that. What was miraculous on earth would be commonplace in heaven.

As we ate, we would talk about the fabulous country we had seen and the fish we had fooled. He would listen attentively and encourage us in our descriptions. We would embellish, never without foundation but still somewhat wildly, and the Lord would grin at us knowingly. Those we loved in life would ask us the questions they knew we couldn't resist. So we would go on, right on the edge of choking we'd be so excited, and talk about the places we hoped to see and the fish we had yet to net. And we would catch our breath and then ask, "Is it possible, Lord? Can it really be? Can it get that good? Will we be able to see and do such things? Will we?"

He will look at us with an almost bemused smile, as a parent does with children so eager and happy they are almost turning themselves inside out, pat us lightly on the shoulder, and say, "My children, you are only beginning to imagine."

PART THREE

My Three Sons
(and New Daughter-in-Law)

The Young Shall Renew Their Hope

I hadn't said anything about it, but I was quite proud of my willpower. For all of those dull miles when Duzzer had been driving and I couldn't doze off, I had resisted all impulses to haul out my stained and wrinkled map of Ontario's Eagle Lake and study the spots I hoped to fish for the first time. I had tried to keep my anticipation from flaming up out of control.

But as Duzzer braked and started to idle through the village of Wabigoon, only forty or forty-five minutes from our lodge on Eagle, I could hold out no longer. I rummaged through my small travel bag and found my map.

"Look at this, guys." I swung around in the copilot's seat and held the map so that Jon, Joel, and Jason in the back of the van could see. "Area 35 — a large bay that looks like the right half of a four-leaf clover. Pretty shallow — most of it probably less than five feet deep. We've never tried it. Been past it a few times, but we've never gone into the bay itself. The map shows lots of vegetation — there are symbols for both submergent and emergent weeds. Weed flats that big should hold a bunch of fish."

"Here we go again," Joel groaned, "Dad and his little pike sanctuaries."

"The bay doesn't look little at all to me." I flipped the map over to find the scale. "If I'm reading this right, the top petal of the clover is probably more than a half mile across, and the one below it is just a tad smaller."

"Dad," Jon closed one of his bird books and responded before Joel could: "Joel doesn't mean the bay is little. He means the pike."

"Huh?" I glanced at Joel, who only shook his head dismissively. "You saying that I have a thing for little pike?"

"Why do you always deny it? Everybody knows that whenever you spot a bay with a bunch of pencil weeds back in it, something draws you into it like a spell. Sure, you catch fish, but they're all little pike. Slimy. Eighteen inches most of them, if that. They hardly deserve to be called hammer-handles. In lots of places on Eagle, anytime anyone makes a cast, he has a chance at a huge musky, the fish of a lifetime. On past trips, especially when we were guided, we caught glimpses of fish like that. But I'm sure the monster-fish places don't include shallow bays with a bunch of reeds growing in the muck — at least not once spawning season is over."

"Anyway," Jason said, grinning, "what's the name of the bay you're talking about?"

"Hmmm, let me check. Didn't notice the name right off. Oh, all right. Here it is. Let's see. . . ." It was a reflex for me to hesitate, because I have a history of pronouncing the names of natural features and towns in ways jarringly unlike the way that those in the know pronounce them. Once in Maine, for instance, my brothers threatened to abandon me on the side of the road after I, talking to a park ranger at an entrance booth to Baxter State Park, called the park's famous mountain not "Ka-TAH-din" but something that could have been used, perhaps in a poem about army dogs serving in the mountains, to rhyme with "Rin Tin Tin." Because others don't usually forget my slips, my relatives often try to play a game with me.

"Look at this new Michigan map I picked up last week," one might say. "See this town on the far west side of the Upper Peninsula? See it? It's spelled O-N-T-O-N-A-G-O-N. Or this one near the tip of the shark's fin just to the east? The one spelled B-E-T-E-Space-G-R-I-S-E? How do you say those?" Back in the days when I trusted them fully, I would take some time pondering, eventually render the name, people sharing genes with me would convulse with laughter, and a family legend would grow by a chapter or two.

Because caustic laughter from anybody, particularly people who are supposed to care about you, is hard on the system, I knew I had to take some time with the name of the weedy bay I had been describing.

It's not the toughest I've ever seen, I mused to myself. Then out loud: "It's K-U-E-N-Z-L-I. I'd say it's 'Keenzly Bay.' Yup. That's it. 'Keenzly Bay.'"

"What?" Joel seemed to be choking. "'Keenzly'! If it was 'Keenzly,' why didn't they spell it the way it sounds? You've got to be kidding me. 'Keenzly Bay.' It could be a lot of things, but it's sure not 'Keenzly.' Who'd ever name a bay like that? Can you just hear it: 'Keenzly Bay,' 'Keenzly Bay,' 'Keenzly Bay'? After a while it gives you a mouth cramp to say it."

"Let me see the map a second," Jason cut in. "Area 35, did you say? I see it — south from Bottleneck Point, right? Boy. I think the bay should be called 'Koonzly.' 'Koonzly' sounds a whole lot better than 'Keenzly.' When we reach camp, we've got to ask Hubie what's right."

"Boys, boys," Duzzer said, using his coach's voice, "do you really think it's worth all the fuss?"

"Let me have a quick look." Jon took the map from Jason. "Hmmm. It wouldn't surprise me if it were 'Kwenzly.' I've seen some words with the *ue* pronounced that way. But I agree — it's not 'Keenzly.'"

"Whoa, whoa, whoa. It's just a name. Jump down my throat, why don't you? And why not all three at once? Goodness gracious alive! The name of one bay among hundreds on a lake among thousands in Ontario. Who needs all this sass? We know there's a bay, we know it's pretty big, we know where it is, we know there's a bunch of weeds in it, we know that weedbeds like that usually hold lots of pike, and we know that at least one of us would like to fish it sometime this week."

What I didn't know then was that when it came to disputes about Kuenzli Bay, the boys and I were just warming up.

After we reached camp, it took only about ten minutes to haul our gear out of the van and lug it into the cabin Hubie assigned us to — all of us knew we had a chance to get out on the water for a few hours yet that night, and we were moving so fast that our main challenge was not plowing into one another. It took the five of us about twice as long to walk over to the main lodge and fill out the forms for our Canadian fishing licenses. And it took us about twice as long as that for Hubie to finish one of his wild stories, this one about fifty-inch muskies tearing into hooked walleyes north of Dog House Reef and making anglers new to Eagle Lake sit down, fight to avoid hyperventilating, and vow never again to wash off their hands in the water.

As we left the main lodge, Duzzer looked up and gave a sharp whistle. "Whoa. Listen to all that commotion in the tops of the trees. Maybe we'd better walk down to the dock and check out how strong the wind is before we gear up."

"Also what direction it's from," Jason added. "Just so it's not from the east. It's always hard to tell up here under all these pines, but it doesn't seem like it's from the east."

As we skidded down the gravel on the slope to the dock area, all of us could see that the wind was up — it was driving waves foaming with silt against the rightmost dock, and as those waves smacked the tires bolted along the edge of that dock, they sent arcs of spray over the dock and into the boats moored on the other side.

"It's pretty strong, but no worse than stuff we've fished in before." Joel was already turning back up toward the cabin.

"True, but it's from the northwest." Duzzer pointed. "The air it's bringing will have some serious bite to it."

I scanned the nearest clouds, some light gray, almost white, others marbled in bluish-black, many with tattered wisps on their trailing edge that looked as if they were about to swirl, come together, and bring slanting shafts of rain, maybe even sleet. "It's a cold front, that's for sure." I pulled a beanie out of my pocket.

"What is it with all the cold fronts?" Duzzer put his back to the wind and tried to get his hood up and tied. "I can't believe it. Someone should just take me out in the woods right now and shoot me. I hate fishing during cold fronts. Why is it that every time I come north to fish I have to travel smack dab into a cold front? Here I go again — fishing with about six layers of clothes on. So many clothes I can hardly make a cast. When did we ever get those pictures of fishing in shorts and T-shirts, anyway? Were we in Canada? Maybe we were only out at Sandy Pines pretending to go for muskies."

"It's not going to be warm and cozy in the boat, that's for sure. And a cold front will knock the fish down. You can sometimes be surprised by one or two, but generally the muskies aren't very active." I was only saying what everyone else was thinking. "But give it some time and you know how it's going to go. After a while the sky will break into cotton-candy clouds with dark bottoms. The wind will gradually shift around to the southwest. As it does, things will warm up and start to get hazy. And by that time, the muskies should start moving again. Maybe this front will go through tonight or to-morrow morning."

In camp we didn't have television, cable or otherwise. The only radio station that came through clearly in the main lodge played country and western nonstop. We didn't think it was worth driving into Dryden to check a newspaper for a weather map. We couldn't check the internet for detailed explanations and forecasts. And no new arrivals in camp brought any useful knowledge with them — all they wanted to talk about was the storms they had driven through. So I can't be sure whether my explanation of the weather during our trip is anywhere close to the truth.

But it seemed to me that as we spent our days rocking and

rolling around Vermillion Bay and the West Arm, searching for spots that would hold a musky that might finally show some interest in our lures, cold front after cold front — seemingly more than one every day — swept down from the northwest and made us think that it would be wise to head for shelter, or at least the lee of an island.

Argue with me all you want. All I know is that I would often look up from the back of our boat to find a new bank of storm clouds churning toward us from the hills cradling Vermillion Bay. And soon after that I would find myself hunched over in the boat, my hands in the pockets of my parka and my head close to my knees, wondering whether the precipitation pummeling my hood and back was just exceptionally heavy rain — some special Canadian rain — or rain with hail pellets mixed in.

And so it was that near the middle of the afternoon on Thursday, our second-to-last day, as we packed up our shore-lunch gear on the small island near Bottleneck Point that we often used for meal stops (we had waited for a break in the rain to eat), I asked the other four: "So what do you think? We've had way too many days in a row with not a single hooked fish. Want to try for something other than muskies? Want to try fighting a pike or two? We're only a half-mile or so away — want to try that bay?"

"What bay you thinking about?" Jason started to rummage in his boat bag for his own map.

"You know. The one I talked about on the drive up — Keenzly Bay."

"That shallow bay you were so hot about?" Joel acted as if it wasn't worth taking me seriously. "You know all we're gonna find in there are some little pike."

"They might be little, but chances are really good that we'll find some fish. It's high time for me to be fighting a fish again, even a little one. I'm not sure I remember what that feels like."

"You know what we always say, Dad," Joel responded. "You can't catch a big fish unless you go where the big fish are. We're up here only one week a year. We've got a day and a half left, and I'm not even close to giving up on a big musky yet. I bet Jon and Jase still have their hopes up, too." He glanced toward Jon and Jason, both of whom nodded in assent, Jason somewhat more eagerly than Jon.

"Well, how about a little compromise?" Duzzer was doing what he sometimes had to do with my sons and me — acting as mediator. "I've got a few spinnerbaits that I haven't even taken out of the package yet this summer. I wouldn't mind hauling a few pike out of the weeds. So why don't we all try that bay, whatever it's called, but let's do it for just fifteen or twenty minutes. It'd be a little break from using all our heavy gear. Sound okay?"

"All right," Jason took over for Joel, "but don't forget what you said — just fifteen or twenty minutes for those slimeskins, and then let's get back to the musky hunt."

"That's fine with me. I just need a little time. I'm on a fishing trip, and I need to feel some life on the end of my line again. You three guys follow Duzzer and me down. When we get to the mouth of the bay, let's get together and decide how we're going to fish it."

As we held our boats side to side and bobbed just outside the mouth of Kuenzli Bay, I glanced first to the south section of the bay. "Look at all those reeds." I pointed. "Over there, all along that shoreline. That's the biggest spread of reeds I've ever seen. And it looks like they stick four or five feet out of the water — some of them are so tall they can't even stand up straight. Let's head over there and fish right in all those reeds."

"Okay, but first check out that shoreline, the one on the west." Jon was standing in their boat and pointing. "Look at those trees, red pines, I think. Twenty-five or thirty of them. Most have lost their tops, but they didn't just crack clean off — the trunks that are left are all wrenched and mangled and hanging down in splinters every which way."

"Goodness gracious. You're right. I hadn't noticed them. Can I borrow your binocs a second?" I stretched from our boat across toward Jon. "Remember that monster storm up here this spring that Hubie talked about? The one that took out all his docks? He said that most of the damage was caused by straight-line winds. But he also heard that a tornado had touched down somewhere on or near the lake; he just wasn't sure where. We haven't seen damage like this anywhere else, so I'm thinking that stand of red pines was hit by the tornado. I don't think I've ever seen tree trunks twisted all up like that — "

"Fine, fine, fine," Joel interrupted, "but do the minutes we're spending here admiring the scenery count in the fifteen or twenty that we agreed on, or do we have to add these on?"

"All right. All right. Let's get to it then." I handed the binoculars back to Jon. "Since we have such a short time, let's take both boats right into the middle of the reeds, and then pooch around near each other casting. We can keep track of who catches the most and the biggest. If we don't have a competition, how will we know who wins?"

We all took out our lighter rods and snapped on spinner-baits. And then the battle of Kuenzli Bay broke out — the action was exactly what I expected it would be on a dark day in a shallow weedy bay. We would flip a spinnerbait down an alley between the reeds, watch it thumping its way back to the boat, and then suddenly it would disappear as a pike flashed out from between some reeds and engulfed it. Sometimes our line would run up on a bent reed, pulling our spinnerbaits right out of the water, and pike would shoot out of the water like miniature Tomahawk missiles, slashing at the dangling skirts. Once Duzzer had a pike hit his spinnerbait, turn, boil in the water, and then shake its head and spit the bait out so hard that it flew back at us and clanged off the side of our boat. Once I was making only a lackadaisical L-turn at the side of the boat when a pike shot from under the motor like a bolt from a crossbow, hit my lure, and almost tore the rod out of my hands. And once Jason, who had put away a spinnerbait and was making short casts with a small minnowbait, giving it erratic little twitches, hooked two pike at the same time, one on the front treble, one on the rear.

If the boys had been ten or twelve years younger, I think they would have completely forgotten any words about time limits and would have welcomed all that pike action. As it was, they did stay at it, with whoops and cackles and outrageous taunts, quite a bit longer than I thought they would, probably for fifty minutes or so. But when I heard Jason say something like "it's just too bad they're all so small," I knew I'd better tell them we could leave if they wanted.

"Okay, guys," I yelled over to them; "thanks for coming along in here. That was great, just what I needed. We can head to the next set of musky spots on your list now if you want."

In fact, that was what they wanted, and they led the way out of the bay.

Four hours later, the five of us sat on the deck of our cabin as I grilled pork chops for our late dinner.

"Those spots we hit the last several hours — those had to be some of the best we've ever fished up here." Jason was marking his map. "At least that's how they looked. I had no idea that bed of cabbage extended so far south from the mouth of McKenzie. Plus I didn't know it was so far off shore. I think we fished inside it last year. Either that or we had the boat right on top of it."

"Good-looking water or not," I said, turning from the grill as the wind shifted momentarily, "we've given this lake more than a fair shot this year, and we still haven't hooked a musky, even a little one. I have half a notion that we should have stayed in Keenzly Bay. That was some real action. We had doubles and triples — one time I thought all five of us were going to have a fish on at the same time, but a couple shook off early. Has anyone ever been a part of a quintuple?"

"Which would all be well and good," Joel said, sounding impatient, "if there were even one or two big fish mixed in with all those babies."

"Well, just because we didn't see any doesn't mean they're not there. I think some of those big mamas everybody talks about could be nestled in there among the weeds. Wouldn't you say so, Duz?"

Jason didn't give him a chance to respond: "Dad, we've been over this and over this. In the spring some of those big fish might use Koonzly Bay to spawn. But I'm positive not a single one of them is in there now."

"What makes you so sure?"

"Well, I can't show you any big scientific studies — if that's what you're looking for. But every time I go guided with Mike and we try a spot and catch a pike, even a decent-sized pike, he starts getting ready to leave. I can almost hear him as he hauls up the trolling motor: 'Okay, reel up — we're outta here.' And you know why? He always says that if a big musky, the kind of musky we're after, happened to be in the area, there wouldn't be any pike around for us to catch. Mike's been fishing up here since he was six years old, and he's thirtysomething now, so I think you can trust what he says about fish in this lake."

"Even if he's right, for me that time catching those pike was as refreshing as any time I've had up here — this year or any past year for that matter. You know, we don't always have to fish the same section of the lake together. Tomorrow we should stay boated up the way we were today. Then you boys can start hitting all your musky spots again, and Duz and I can head back to Keenzly for a spell. It doesn't have to be long. Just long enough to catch a dozen or so. Maybe we should even start the day out there. Once we've actually fought some of those, it'll seem easier to make our million casts for muskies. Sound okay to you, Duz?"

"I don't have a problem with that. We can give the bay a shot and still have plenty of time for the spots where we've seen muskies in the past."

"But Dad," Joel objected, "what's the big deal with those little pike? I don't get why you're so fascinated with those fish."

"Well, for one thing, I have a ton of absolutely great memories of you and your brothers catching pike, usually little pike, when you were all really young. And now when I'm hooking into pike like that, even if it's fifteen years later or so, those great memories start to play in my head."

"I don't remember catching any pike when I was really little," Jon mused. "I got some good ones when you took T-Gunz and me up to Les Cheneaux. I think one of my fish even won third place in the weekly contest up there. Worth fifty bucks, maybe seventy-five. But that wasn't when I was really little — that was for my eighth-grade graduation."

"Well, at one point you did catch a little pike, and it was when you were only about eight years old. And as a matter of fact it was at Les Cheneaux, but not during the trip with T-Gunz. It was the first trip any of us ever took up to Snows Channel. All five of us. And Grandpa and Grandma came along. They set up their trailer across the road from our cottage. Remember?"

"It's kinda fuzzy."

"Well, the first night we were up there, right after supper, Grandpa, you, and I loaded up the boat that came with the cottage and headed out to try for some pike."

"Grandpa came out in the boat with us?"

"Yeah, that was before he got sick of rocking around in the waves and started sitting on the dock all the time. Anyway, to tell the truth, the three of us really had no clue. We didn't know where to fish, most of our equipment wouldn't have been heavy enough to handle a big pike, and we didn't know what would be best to use for bait — that was before we learned those tricks with frozen smelt. Plus I wasn't sure how that fourteen-foot boat was going to handle in the waves of some of those bigger bays. So we ended up tucking into a little cove in Duck Bay —

just south around a couple of points from our cottage — and then for each of us I hooked up a sucker minnow, attached a big bobber about three feet above the hook, and lobbed the bobber and bait toward the reeds along the shore. The thing was, no sooner had we all gotten bait in the water than you spotted a great blue heron."

"I knew what a great blue heron was?"

"You acted like you knew. But it couldn't have been an adult, because it was only about a foot and a half tall, and its size seemed to be helping it. It was poised among some short reeds along one of the sandy spits at the head of the cove, and it was nabbing minnows, one every five seconds or so, almost like clockwork. The minnows probably thought it was just a reed a little fatter and grayer than usual. Anyway, you were counting the minnows as the heron swallowed them, and then Grandpa said, 'Jon, you might want to think about setting your hook. Your bobber is heading straight out into the big bay, and I don't think that sucker all by itself can drag a big bobber like that. At least not that fast.'"

"So I was the first with any action?"

"You were also the first one I helped get bait in the water. Anyway, you gave your line a jerk about as hard as you could give, there was this boil in the water, you had to reel like mad when the fish started swimming straight at you — for a while I thought you worried you lost it — it ran straight under the boat, you finally managed to pull it back toward you and to the deep-water side of the boat, after it dove twice you got its head up slightly, and Grandpa stabbed at it, stabbed at it with the net, almost knocked the fish off your line, and then finally got it. That was the only fish we caught that night. In fact, we didn't even have any false alarms. And when we headed back and were gliding toward the dock, where Joel and Jason were fishing and Mom and Grandma were sitting in chairs waiting for us, you stood up in the bow, pumped your arms in the air, and yelled 'I got one! I got a fish! I got a pike! A fifteen-incher! My biggest fish ever! You should have seen it! It had teeth! Grandpa netted it for me! And Dad got it off the hook. Mom, I got a big one!' That was as excited and happy as I've ever seen you in your life. You were doing some crazy little dance in the bow of the boat. If you had been bigger, you might have tipped us over."

"I do remember that now, at least most of it." Jon brushed the back of his hand across his mouth. "So what about Joel and Jason? Are your memories of them from Les Cheneaux, too?"

"My memory of Jason is. But not from exactly the same spot."

"I remember catching perch and rock bass off the dock at Les Cheneaux, hundreds of them. I even got this huge dogfish once." Jason gave the dry little cough he gets when he's been in too much wind over water. "But I don't remember any pike from when I was little."

"How about this: Do you remember that one day you boys and I drove over to the harbor in Hessel? I'm not sure whether it was during our very first trip up there or not, but I know Grandpa and Grandma were along."

"I kinda remember that. Didn't that harbor have a bunch of floating wooden docks coming off the big cement piers?"

"Yeah, and we fished off just about every one of those docks that didn't have a boat tied up to it. The neatest thing, though, was the bait we used."

"Smelt?"

"No. When we first walked out on the outermost cement pier, one of you guys happened to notice that there were small underwater clouds of little shiner minnows in the water on the inside of the piers. So we rigged up a couple of our lightest poles with the smallest hooks we could find — put a speck of rolled-up bread crust from our lunch on the hooks, and then caught half a pail-full of those shiners. Then we hooked them just under the dorsal, used the lightest bobber we had that would suspend them, tossed them out from the end of some of those wooden docks — we put out two rods for each of us — wedged the rods between planks, set the reel to free spool, and waited."

"Were there a couple of big cabin cruisers docked across from us?" Jason seemed to be remembering things.

"Absolutely huge. And in one of them, I remember, people were sitting out on the back deck and watching if we would catch anything. And they didn't have to wait very long. You were way down on the east end, keeping an eye on a couple of bobbers. Then I heard you yelling: 'Dad, Dad, this bobber is three feet under the water. It's heading across toward that boat.' 'Grab the rod and yank on it!' I yelled; 'set the hook.' 'Me?' you yelled back. 'Yes, you! You're the only one over there. Set it, set it! I'm on my way.' So you grabbed the rod, gave a big sweeping motion, and as I got close to you, the rod started to throb. 'Help, Dad, help,' you panted; 'it's way too heavy.' 'Naw, Jase, you can get it. You can get it. Just pull steady. Keep the pressure on. That's it. There you go. I've got the net ready. Bring that baby in. I think you're gonna get your first pike ever. Just bring it in smooth and steady.' And then I saw this huge mass of weeds, a bushel-basket-full of weeds, and I thought, 'No, not a bunch of weeds. Make it not be just a big pulled-out snag.' But as you leaned back one last time and brought those weeds close enough for me to slide the net under the whole mess, I caught a glimpse of the head of a pike, and once we sorted everything out, we found that you had caught weeds and snails weighing at least twelve pounds and a northern pike weighing one or two."

"But I got it in all by myself?"

"Yup, and as I helped you release the fish, you just started to gurgle."

"That was cool. What I remember best, though, was that the people in the cabin cruiser across the way actually stood up, came to the rail, and started to clap."

"That's when you really surprised me."

"How so?"

"Well, I'm not sure where you got it from, probably from some preschool play or something, but you very calmly put one arm behind your lower back and the other across your stomach and then you bowed across the water toward those spectators. I could hardly believe it, but you did this perfect little formal bow."

"I didn't learn it in preschool — it was in kindergarten. We had a student teacher that year who tried a writing workshop with us, and any time one of us would read to the class or show what we had drawn and the class would applaud, we were supposed to stand up and give a little bow. So it was no big deal for me to bow to those people on the boat."

"Maybe not, but they went crazy — they started to hoot and slap the railing on their boat they liked it so much. Before that I didn't know you had so much of the show-off in you."

"I wasn't really showing off. Giving a little bow just seemed like the right thing to do. So what about Joel? What's your memory of little pike and Joel?"

"Can't be one." Joel was stretching his legs out. "Can't be one because I never messed with fish like that in my life."

"Oh yes you did," I countered; "and as a matter of fact, the pike I remember you for was probably the smallest pike anyone in our family has ever caught."

"You've gotta be kidding. And I suppose it happened up at Les Cheneaux for me too."

"Nope. Not at Les Cheneaux. But in the Upper Peninsula. Just a ways to the west."

"Where? I sure don't remember doing any other fishing in the U.P."

"One time we camped for a week at Indian Lake State Park. We spent some of our time on the beach there, but we also made some modest trips to areas around the park. We went to the big spring, which had huge brown trout swimming in it, and we showed you boys Fayette, where I remember you couldn't believe the gigantic carp in the harbor. And one afternoon we drove over to Seney and fished in some of the pools in the wildlife refuge. They had a two-track that led along the tops of the dikes and over narrow wooden bridges, and every so often, we found pathways worn down through the weeds and reeds to the water. Well, at one point I parked along the dike and Jon and Jason and I went down one of those little pathways and I got them set up to cast Baby One-minuses out toward what looked like floating pads of boggy vegetation. You decided it would be too crowded for four of us to stand in that spot, so you went back up to the top of the dike and headed off to find a pathway of your own."

"How old was I then?"

"I'm not sure. Maybe I could check some of Mom's old photo albums to find out. She usually wrote the date on the back of each picture. But you were awfully small, I remember that much. The reeds along the dike where we parked were way over your head." And to myself I mused, *He couldn't have been eight or nine. That must have been before the night when he thought Wanda and I abandoned him.*

"So I took off and found my own place to fish?"

"Yeah, there we all were, Jon and Jason and I at the water's edge of one pathway, Mom up walking around checking out butterflies on the top of the dike, and you off out of sight down your own pathway. And then I heard you screaming for me: 'Dad! Dad! I need help! Hurry! Dad, where are you?' So I scrambled back to the top of the dike and tried to figure out where you were, where your yelling was coming from. But the wind was swirling and I couldn't tell for sure and I ran down the way we had come for fifty yards or so and didn't see you and so I sprinted back to the car and a bit beyond and then stopped and listened some more but you weren't yelling anymore and I had no idea which way from the car you must have gone and I was really starting to get scared. And then from about thirty yards out in front of the car you popped onto the top of the dike from among the reeds and started walking back to the car, holding something with both hands. 'A picture,' you demanded; 'you've got to get a picture.' And there you were, with your hands close to each other and thrust out toward me, hands holding a pike so small that only about two inches of its head showed to the right of your hands and two inches of its tail showed to the left. That thing had to be only twelve or thirteen inches long. But you posed for a picture, and that pose has always seemed to me to be one of the proudest I've ever seen you in — one foot out in front of the other, your head tilted back, your lips in a huge pucker."

"I don't remember all that, but I do remember standing there hidden in all those reeds and hooking that fish just three feet or so from my feet. It scared me since it came from the side. Hard. I don't think I saw it until it had turned with my spinnerbait in its mouth. I was yelling since I didn't think I could unhook it, but as I stepped away from the water and held it up by the line, it shook like mad, came right off the hook, and landed on the bank."

"Yup. Jon dancing in that little aluminum boat, Jason bowing to strangers across the water, Joel posing on top of that dike. I hope you can see what I mean when I say I have great memories of you three guys and little pike. And any time I catch a little pike, I almost feel the way I felt as a proud young dad. I really feel that way at times like this afternoon, when you guys are actually right there near me."

"I can see why you like those memories," Jason conceded; "it was cool just hearing about them. But we're not those little guys anymore. And now what we're after is big muskies. I'd call that progress. Just think of the memories you'd have if you were with us when we landed a fifty-incher."

"No one knows better than I that you're not those little guys anymore. I think of that every time I see anybody taking a little kid out in a boat. And although I've already got memories of big fish, more would be great. But it doesn't seem as if any of us is going to make those kinds of memories this week, does it? Just think back over these past few days. One or two days nobody in either boat saw a single musky. And when we did have follows, they were always really lazy. We haven't even had a single musky nipping at a bait. Well, I'm sorry, but I'm not used to going on fishing vacations and not catching any fish. I certainly didn't come a thousand miles to get skunked. I could drive a lot less and get skunked. What do I do back at the office, say 'Oh, we didn't catch anything, but we had about a half-dozen follows'? Someone there is bound to figure out that those are pretty expensive follows. Like I said before, every so often I need to feel some life on the other end of my line. I could probably even handle it if every so often a musky would come hard after my lure, hit at the boat, and then shake itself loose during a tail dance. But just a handful of lazy follows! When it's that way for days, it's hard for me to keep my hope up. I start to wonder if I'm ever going to catch anything again. And I hate that — casting, casting, casting, and not really expecting a fish to hit. And I think that Duzzer also has felt like that at times this week. Isn't that right, Duz?"

"I didn't want to make a big deal of it because I like coming up here so much, just seeing this water and country and all, and we've certainly had some good years on this lake, but yeah, pretty much I've felt like that this week."

"Yeah, so that's why I think Duzzer and I will spend the first half hour or so tomorrow in Keenzly Bay. It's like we have this sure thing on the lake waiting for us, something we can depend on no matter how tough the fishing is everywhere else. So after we've fought a bunch of fish in Keenzly Bay in the morning, it won't seem so bad ending the trip casting for musky and seeing only a lazy follow or two. If that."

"Okay," Joel responded. "It's your vacation. Spend it how you want. Just don't ask us to fish that bay with you."

"Well, if we don't see you on the water tomorrow, just remember that you can't fish straight through to dark. We have to be back at the cabin no later than eight so that we can eat and then get as much packed up as possible. On Saturday morning we don't want to have to do much more than grab some breakfast, climb in the van, and hit the road."

If other anglers had been sitting around with us on the deck of our cabin that night, I can almost predict how they would have judged what I said: "He doesn't seem to know it, but he's going to be wrong, dead wrong. He's assuming that he and his friend will once again have some wild action for pike in Kuenzli Bay and then for the whole rest of the day will see nothing more than a lazy musky follow. But he's going to be wrong. Everybody knows there's no sure thing in fishing; it's as unpredictable as the weather. All the pike in Kuenzli Bay could very well drop out of the bay into deeper water overnight. And even in some not-very-fishy-looking spot a pig of a musky might come hot after one of their baits and eat it at boatside."

They could think such thoughts all they wanted; if they had been on our deck, they might even have dropped some hints about them to me. But as it turned out, I was right about every detail of the last day on Eagle for Duzzer and me. From camp in the morning, we motored directly down to Kuenzli, where each of us, in less than an hour, caught more pike that we could keep track of. I'm not kidding. I started out trying to keep an accurate count, but somewhere after nine or ten I lost count. Probably around twenty, I think, is what I ended up with. And they all weren't tiny — some had to be close to twenty-five or twenty-six inches.

Plus after we left the bay, we took our musky hunt seriously. We tried lots of good-looking spots, we tried all of our proven lures, we almost certainly made hundreds of casts, and we varied our retrieves in every way that we knew of. But we didn't see a single musky. We didn't even see some shadow or flash that we could have claimed was a musky. And not once did we see the boys, so we couldn't find out if they were doing any better.

So if I hadn't been able to draw some strength from the smugness that comes with being right about the day, I would have been exhausted by the time Duzzer and I pulled up back at the dock.

The boys had beaten us back, and they must have done so by several minutes, because they already had most of their gear stacked on the dock and were just lolling in the seats of their boat.

"I've got to light some fire under them." I hopped onto the dock; "we've got too much packing to do yet for them to be lollygagging in their boat." As I walked over to them, my back gradually loosened up — "way too much standing up today with a bum hip," I thought. As I came up to their boat, Joel and Jason were watching me closely, and Jon was focusing on the screen of the slick little camcorder that Jason had bought to use on fishing trips. "What are you guys up to? Why are you just sitting around? You know we have a ton of work to do yet tonight. Why haven't you started lugging your equipment up to the cabin?"

"Just dial it down a little, Dad." Jon held the camcorder out to me. "Do you want to see some of the great scenery we found today? There's a rockslide in a part of the lake we're pretty sure you've never been to, and it's unbelievable. The rocks carried trees with them right down toward the water, and some of them were snapped like matchsticks while others still seem to be growing — sideways, down, up, every which way. Want a look?"

"Okay, a quickie, and then we've got to get moving."

"Just push that red button on the top. No, the one to the right. There you go. I've already rewound it for you." Jon had something in his voice that I couldn't identify.

Immediately after I pushed the correct button, I couldn't make sense of what I was seeing. I blinked twice, hard, and then realized that I was looking at someone's skinny backside, about three inches of boxer shorts showing above dark warm-up pants. After a few more seconds I could tell that what I was seeing was Jason kneeling in the bow of their boat, with his upper body bent over the side and both of his arms extending down into the water.

"What?" I pressed the pause button and looked over to the boys. "What's going on? I thought you said something about scenery. Did Jason get sick today or something? You actually made a video of him losing his lunch in the lake? Come on."

"Just turn it back on and keep watching." Jon gave me a slight backhanded wave. "Watch some more."

I hit the button again. And then I saw Jason slowly straighten up from his waist, start to draw both of his arms up, raise a knee and methodically bring first one foot under him and then the other, stand up while hauling something from the water, and finally pivot to face the camera, proudly displaying a monster musky, probably about fifty inches long. "Oh, my goodness gracious! You guys! You guys! 'Want to see some great scenery?' Sure. Trick me like that someday and I'm going to have a heart attack. But Jay, that thing is gorgeous, absolutely gorgeous. Where did you ever nail it? Duzzer and I didn't see a thing today, not a single thing."

"Do you know that pinkish boulder that sticks out of the water near the mouth of McKenzie Bay? On the south side?"

"Yeah. It's before you get to the little island where the terns always seem to nest, isn't it? You weren't all that far from Duzzer and me, at least when we were in Keenzly Bay."

"Maybe so. Well, whenever we're around McKenzie with Mike the guide, he tells us about all the huge muskies he's pulled from around that boulder. He says he's caught more than thirty muskies from that one little spot, and I guess I always thought he was blowing smoke in our faces, but today when I tossed my Cisco Bulldawg as close to the boulder as I dared, the bait hit the surface and settled for maybe a second, and then it came blasting straight up out of the water. This musky must have hit it with its snoot, and the bait went flying five or six feet in the air. I wasn't even sure what all was going on, so I just started reeling, reeling as fast as I could turn the handle, and I could tell I didn't have a dawgball because the lure was coming through the water just fine, and when it got about fifteen feet from the boat I could see a big wake right behind it and then a second or two later this huge mouth opened up and took it all in. You should have seen it. One second there was this cream-colored bait coming at me with its tail fluttering like mad and the next it was gone, totally gone, swallowed."

"How did you ever fight that thing? Didn't that first hit almost stun you?"

"For a few seconds I was almost numb. First that bulldawg went flying in the air, then I saw the wake, and then this huge mouth opened up and inhaled the bulldawg. But at least I was able to keep pressure on the fish, and Jon and Joel helped a lot. Jon lifted the trolling motor out of the way, and Joel netted the fish before it was able to run under the boat."

"When did this all happen?"

Jon took over for Jason: "It's weird, really. We had just mentioned that we only had about twenty minutes left to fish before we had to head in. And then Jason made that cast to the boulder."

"What about earlier in the day? Did you see any? Hook any?"

Joel gave a little hmmph: "You know, Dad, that was the only action we had. Up until Jase's fish, we didn't have a single hit. And we didn't see anything either."

"You put in all those hours on the water with absolutely no action until this fish? And you kept at it hard? Did you at least take a little break for a snack? Or fish for something else for a change?"

"What else is there?" Joel shrugged. "We kept at it pretty hard. You should know by now that it takes more than ten or eleven hours to make us give up on muskies."

"That's just plain unbelievable to me. Duzz and I fished hard for muskies today too, but we started out with a bunch of pike, and after I had fought them, it didn't bother me so much just to be washing lures."

"Well, if you ever start to wonder, Dad," Joel said, using the voice I had heard him use as a summer-camp counselor, "just ask us. We know just about all there is to know about hope."

"You're kinda young for that, but if you say so, I might try to believe you. I've got to check your recording out one more time. How far should I rewind it? Where does it start? Back to 2:33? Okay, let's see how close I can come. Oops. Went back too far. I'll just start it there. What is this — an eagle? That's a bald eagle. What a great shot. We've seen lots of eagles up here, but that one is really close. How'd you ever get so close? And where was this, anyway?"

"Should have rewound it yourself, Jon," Joel muttered.

"That?" Jon looked over my shoulder. "Oh, yeah, that's a bald eagle we saw just before we moved to McKenzie and Jason got his fish. I didn't have my camera along, so I got it with Jason's camcorder. Just fast-forward through that and you'll get to where Jason is getting ready to lift his fish out of the water. We were all too busy to get any of the fight on tape."

"Just a second. The picture of that eagle's a stunner. I've got to pause this a second — I thought I noticed something." The eagle was in the very center of the picture frame, perched on a horizontal branch completely stripped of its bark, peering off to the right, a few of its breast feathers raised by a breeze. Just behind the magnificent bird, partly obscured by its body, were several long and twisted splinters, extending down and out of the frame to the left, apparently all that was left of a red pine's crown.

The Spirit Is Willing

When my three sons were young, ranging in age from five to ten, whatever success they ever had as anglers was due almost entirely to me. I picked the lakes we towed our boat to. On those lakes, I chose the spots that looked best for panfish, bass, or pike. While preparing to fish those spots, I snapped on all lures and hooked up all live bait. Plus there was never a rat's nest in a line that I didn't untangle. There was never a netted fish that I didn't unhook. And there was never a plastic worm accidentally tossed onto part of some docked pontoon boat that I didn't retrieve, apologizing profusely if the owners happened to be near enough to notice what was going on.

As my sons grew into their late teens and early twenties, the four of us began to explore the adrenaline-washed realm of musky fishing. In my view, this was almost entirely a good thing. The only drawback about musky fishing with my sons was that by the time we started catching freshwater fish about four feet long, those sons asserted themselves so strongly and became so competitive as anglers that I wondered whether I would be able to stay ahead of them or even just keep up with them.

For one thing, it took them hardly any time at all to learn an impressive amount about muskies and musky fishing. They read every article they could find, they bought several DVDs, they attended musky seminars at fishing shows, and they started e-mailing anglers prominent in the musky world. They discovered what kinds of rods worked best with what kinds of lures, and they did research on the retrieve ratios of different reels. They heard through various grapevines what lures were being developed by tackle companies, and they found out who the prominent independent lure makers were and started ordering custom-made baits — signed, dated, and numbered. Beyond all that, they learned the names of what seemed to be all the lakes in the upper Midwest where muskies lived. Their knowledge extended so far that they could list the names of successful guides on the Ottawa River, on the several large flowages in northern Wisconsin, and on big Minnesota lakes like Mille Lacs and Vermillion.

I thought that at some point I could probably catch up to them in knowledge; I just would have to use my time a little differently than I ever had previously. The more serious issue was that by the time we all started chasing muskies, I was approaching sixty years of age, and I wasn't sure I could meet the physical demands of hunting these elusive fish, especially when I saw what kind of gear my sons were having the most success with.

They were using eight and a half- and nine-foot rods. These, they said, had enough backbone to handle strong and heavy fish, and they allowed them to make wide and smooth figure eights or circles at boatside to entice fish into eating. When I first saw one of these rods, it reminded me of the equipment a middle-school track coach had held up as he tried to persuade me that I had a body "perfectly made for the pole vault."

And the lures my sons had the most success with — my goodness, these lures were huge, heavy, and hard to reel in. For example, the boys caught lots of fish on Magnum or even Pounder Bull Dawgs. After I spent some time hoisting these behind me and then launching them out over the water, parts that I never knew I had in my shoulder started to grind against one another. After fishing, I could move my shoulder around, and that joint would make clearly audible clicking sounds.

My sons caught even more fish on double-ten-blade bucktails. After some sessions of casting these, I developed such acute tendinitis in my right elbow that for a time I could barely hold a fork at dinner. If I were to stick with such lures, I worried that I would have to take so much ibuprofen that I would probably die of some liver disease before old age would assert its claim on me.

But then one summer in a cove off the backchannel of Eagle Lake, I learned something that promised to help me hold my own with my sons in the hunt for trophy fish. All four of us were being guided by Cal from Andy Myers Lodge. To that point we had had a great day — four muskies to forty-nine inches in the net — and we were trying a few more spots before heading back to the dock. As we prepared to fish that cove, Joel decided it was time to try a new lure. He took off the Martian double 10 he had been using most of the day. And he put on a lure that we mocked him for. It was a surface lure — a Super Turbo — with a respectable enough shape, but its colors were totally unnatural and clearly outrageous — its body was purple and its two small propellers were pink.

"What draws muskies to this place?" I asked Cal. "It doesn't look as deep as most places we've been fishing. And no rocks that I can see."

"Two clusters of what we call 'tobacco cabbage' in here. One just ahead of us and another pretty close to the mid — "

And then Joel lurched backwards a step and rocked the boat violently, his reel gave off a *whaeet* as his line exploded from the spool in tangled whorls, he thrust his rod into the sky and then jerked it back at a sharp angle, Cal yelled "Still on?" as he jostled his way past me toward Joel, Joel yelled back "Yah, yah, yah, but my reel's fried," and then Cal grabbed the line and he and Joel pulled the hooked forty-five-inch musky hand over hand into the net that Jon, my oldest, had extended.

After Cal had unhooked the fish and we all had snapped some pictures, I kept Joel from a complete basking in glory by firing several questions at him:

"So, with those prop-style surface baits, all you do is reel straight in?"

"Yup."

"You don't have to twitch them or rip them or anything?"

"Nope."

"And it doesn't look as if the reeling is too hard."

"Naw, about the easiest musky lure to reel there is. Reel 'em all day and feel no pain."

"No pain would be great. And do surface lures work in lots of conditions, even in waves?"

"Absolutely. I've had fish attack this lure when I was rocking around so badly I could hardly stand up."

"And how about different times of the year?"

"Maybe not the absolute best really early and late. But most of the time they're good; they just flat out catch fish. And the strikes are usually as dramatic as they come."

I'm saved, I thought. *I could order a bunch of surface baits and toss them* without grinding up my shoulder or going numb in my right arm below the elbow. With baits like these, maybe I could fish as long and hard and well as my sons, not just be dead weight in the back of the boat munching pretzels.

Shortly after we got back to Michigan, on a stiflingly humid afternoon just before a strong cold front was supposed to come slamming through, Jason and I headed out to Campau Lake, the musky lake closest to our home. We were fishing off the outside weed edge in twelve to fourteen feet of water, Jason using a gold double 10 while I was trying a new Pacemaker. For the first hour or so, we saw nothing. As we fished our way across the tip of a long underwater bar, however, I suddenly noticed something different near my lure as it approached the boat.

"Look, Jase," I hissed, "there's a bulge behind the Pacemaker; it's like a big shoulder of water."

"It's a follow, Dad, a pretty hot follow. It's right on it. Speed it up. C'mon, speed it up. Now a smooth L-turn. Make it smooth, Dad, and that baby will hit."

Just as I began to make out the fish below the bulge of water, I went into my L-turn — smooth, smooth, smooth, the propeller churning and leaving a pronounced bubble trail as I took the lure subsurface.

But the musky got to within a few feet of us and then turned parallel to the boat and vanished into the dark.

"What's the deal? That was smooth. I didn't mess that up; I know I didn't."

"You couldn't do anything about that, Dad. Your L-turn was

one of your better ones ever. Something spooked it. Maybe it saw the boat. Nothing you can do about that. Just keep casting."

I did, and two casts later, when the Pacemaker was about halfway back to the boat, a musky came from straight below it, missed the bait entirely, flew about three feet into the air, did a twisting somersault with beads of water shimmering off in every direction, and crashed back into the lake.

"Goodness gracious alive! Did you see that, Jase? It missed. Somehow it missed my bait. How could it miss like that? I thought these deserved to be called predators. And I wasn't even reeling that fast. Whew! — I've got to get my heart rate down! Can you believe that? Two fish in less than two minutes? These surface baits might not always get them hooked, but they sure get their attention and stir them up."

"It's maybe a little surprising, but muskies do miss sometimes. You should see them go airborne when they miss my Weagle. They must take aim and set their course, and when I twitch it out of their course, they just fly right past. But come on — get your lure back out there."

"Okay, but three fish in just a few minutes would be almost unbelievable."

I cast, and as soon as the Pacemaker landed, it seemed that someone dropped a boulder into the water near it.

"Keep reeling, Dad." Jason's voice went falsetto. "It attacked but it's not on. Keep reeling. It'll follow. It's going to eat; it's going to eat. Fast. Faster!"

I made that Pacemaker cough and sputter — it was the picture of desperation — but nothing hit it, and as it approached the boat, I could see no following fish either.

"I can't believe that. Three fish in a few minutes either attacking or thinking of attacking and not one of them on the hook. It's like I've got fish from all over the lake chasing this lure, but then none of them actually hits. I can't remember when I've had action like this. Now all I need is to hook one."

And then with a little "ungh," Jason, who had been burning his double 10, reared back and yelled "fish!"

And he was right. He kept the fish from going into the air, I put my rod down and grabbed the net, he turned the fish and got its head up, he led it back toward me, and it ended up being a fat forty-six-incher, with gorgeous spots, especially ahead of its tail. In the picture that I snapped, Jason's smile is broad and confident, almost cocky, with just a hint of wryness.

By the time we had released the fish, it was deep dusk, and we decided to head home. When we got there and I was lugging my gear into the basement, Wanda turned from the memory book she was working on and asked, "Get anything?"

"You can't believe it," I put down my tackle bag. "You know I'm using some kind of surface lure almost all the time now, and I had incredible action. Three fish in three or four minutes. It was like there was a whole pack of muskies out there that I drove nuts with that clacking retrieve. I mean absolutely nuts! First a follow, then an airborne miss, and then an all-out attack."

"But did you hook any of them?"

"Naw. Stupid fish. Not a single one ate my bait. You'd think at least one of the three would have eaten. But just a minute after all that action, Jase got one on his double 10. Forty-six-incher. He'll tell you about it in a minute. He's outside hooking up the battery charger. Time for me to hit the shower."

When I got out of the shower and had cracked the door to vent some steam, I realized that Jason and Wanda were talking in the next room. When I turned off the exhaust fan, I could just make out their words:

"But are you sure, Jase?"

"I'm pretty sure, Mom. Dad thinks he ran into this huge school of muskies and got them all riled up with his Pacemaker. First a hot follow, then a miss that went straight up, and then an attack from the side. But I got pretty good looks each time. I'm almost sure it was the same fish. It wanted to eat and missed his bait three separate times but then eventually found and ate my bucktail."

"But can you say for absolute certain it was the same fish?"

"Not for absolute certain. But pretty sure."

"Well, that's important; pretty sure is not certain. I wouldn't want any lies or deceit. But don't forget that your dad turned sixty not too long ago. And in most ways he's handled that okay. Still, you know how he's always been when it comes to fishing with you boys."

"Everybody who knows him knows that."

"So since you can't be positive it wasn't a bunch of different fish, I think it would be best to let him keep on believing what he already believes."

Not a Hair Shall Fall

"**Y**ear after year lately — I must be jinxed." It was Jon, barely audible above the radio.

Joel, Jason, Duzzer, and T-Gunz were all in various states of restless dozing in the back of our rented van as we tried to make it back from northwest Ontario to Grand Rapids in one numbingly long travel day. Jon had volunteered to stay awake and sit up front with me as I put in a shift as driver. I was glad for his company: as we started the gradual climb out of Thunder Bay with hopes of making no stops until Marathon or maybe even White River, I knew that he would be quicker than I to spot any moose approaching the pavement and that he would find enough to talk about so that I wouldn't nod off and miss one of the sharp turns through rock cuts on the Trans-Canada Highway.

That Jon would want to do some troubles talk didn't surprise me. He was in a relationship with a young woman who was wonderful in many ways but who flinched at the mere mention of the word commitment. But I certainly didn't expect to hear about jinxes from a son in his late teens.

"Jinxed? What do you mean? You been reading too much Harry Potter lately?"

"I wish this were fiction. But it's not. I've been trying like mad the last few years, but I just can't catch a really big fish."

"Hold on a second. You've caught just about the biggest fish of anyone in our family — that monster catfish you got out of Muskegon Lake. Don't you remember how that thing almost destroyed our net and how you and I together had trouble lifting it?"

"That seems like a lifetime ago — I was just a kid. I'm talking about the last few years of fishing, especially our trips to Canada. Besides, on that day I wasn't even trying for catfish. I was fishing for pike and happened to hook a flathead. Uncle Brian says he's fished the Grand River for cats, but none of us has ever tried for them. You know that. Give us a choice, and we go after pike and muskies every time — we've got the fever, and everyone says that people with the fever never get well enough to wonder about a cure."

"Maybe, but I'm guessing that their relatives do. Anyway, it sure seems to me that both in Canada and around West Michigan over the past several years you've gotten into fish pretty well, especially the pike. At least when you're not meditating or taking pictures."

"Well, pretty good numbers some days but never anything really big. I'm talking about something forty inches long or longer. I'm positive that everyone else in this van right now has gotten at least one fish like that — Jason can put in five minutes of casting on some little dock and catch one — but all that ever happens to me is that I get to where I think I finally have a chance to nail one, and then I get shut out. Nothing ever goes my way."

"This is just fishing, Jon — you learn all you can, stay on

good water as much as possible, make your casts, and then wait to see what happens. It's a matter of patience and hope. Why would you say that nothing goes your way?"

"Do you remember the first time we fished Little Vermillion Lake up by Sioux Lookout?"

"Sure."

"And do you remember the day when you and Joel took that hike to Booger Lake and fished from one of the boats stashed there?"

"Absolutely. I remember all my days on the water, but that's one of those with a special frame around it. Practically as soon as Joel and I pushed off from shore, we found a thick bed of cabbage. On Joel's very first cast he caught a pike, not a big one, about twenty-eight inches, but a real dervish. Almost came tail first right into the boat with us. And then on his second cast he hooked into another pike. But this was a big one, one that knew lots of tricks."

"That's the kind of fish I'm talking about."

"Fortunately, by that age Joel had learned how to be patient with a fish. He fought him smart and won. We didn't have a measuring tape along, but that fish had to be over forty inches. Joel's hands were shaking so much that I had to help him un-hook it. After that we went about twenty minutes with no ac-tion at all. But then — I'll never forget how it happened — Joel was standing in the bow, burning a spinnerbait over the tops of the cabbage, when I asked him about the upcoming soccer sea-son. He turned toward me and started bragging about how he thought his team had a great chance to win the state champion-ship; then he glanced back to check his lure as it approached the boat and saw a monster pike — maybe not quite as long as the first one that day but thicker in the shoulders — that came on a diagonal and ate his bait. Very calmly, almost methodically. But when that fish felt the hook, it went nuts — thrashing on the surface and then diving away from us into the weeds. Once it was in the weeds, Joel couldn't budge it. And he started to worry about losing it. Every look he gave me was pure desperation. But we moved the boat around and pulled that fish out of the weeds from the back side. When Joel posed for a quick picture, he looked like the prince of all portages."

"Joel's still got that picture above his bed. What you probably don't remember about that day is that early that morning I was thinking of going along. But I also wanted to fish the reef near Pete's Island on the upper arm of Little Vermillion, and decided to stay behind with Jason to give it a shot. We never saw a single fish. So when you and Joel got back, Joel almost turning himself inside out with all his bragging, I was really ticked that I hadn't gone along. You must have noticed because you said you'd be happy to hike back to Booger the next day with whoever wanted to go along. Joel wanted to go back, and I wanted to get into something like what he had caught, so the three of us trekked back there a day later. But we never raised a single big fish. All we could do was get some little pike to slash at our spinnerbaits as they clattered through pencil reeds. I know it seemed like fun, but for me it was pure frustration."

"I thought it was great, and I wasn't even fishing half the time — mainly I was watching you and Joel. Don't you remember the times when one of your spinnerbaits would get hung up out of the water on a bent reed and a pike would blast right out of the water after it? Hardly any of them got on the hook, but those aerial attacks were some of the coolest things I've ever seen. You telling me you didn't enjoy that, even a little?"

"After Joel had gotten those two big pike the day before, you don't know how badly I wanted one myself, but I was a day late. As usual."

"Let's not turn these days into a big deal. Don't you remember what the weather was like then? Check whatever pictures we have if you don't believe me. The first day, the clouds kept thickening up until we were under a heavy overcast. And it was so humid and hazy that it almost felt like we were sitting in a sauna. Kind of hard to breathe. You know that on those days pike often go nuts. Some of that weather was still around early the next morning, but by the time the three of us made it all the way back to Booger, the day had turned into a bluebird special — no haze, postcard clouds, wind from the northwest. The thing is, when you're sitting in a fishing camp, who knows ahead of time what the weather for the next day is going to be like? One of the reasons I go on fishing trips is to get away from news reports. You just happened to miss the great weather by a day. Big deal. It was a fluke of changing weather patterns."

"A fluke? If that was a fluke, then my days, especially my recent days fishing in Canada, are one fluke right after another."

"Almost constant flukes? Is that even logically possible? You've got to watch what you say. People working toward English majors are supposed to be more careful with their language. I bet you can't give me even one other so-called example."

"Are you kidding? I could come up with dozens."

"I'll settle for one. Let's hear it."

"Okay, but this is way too easy for me. You remember that day the second year on Little Vermillion when you and Duzzer and T-Gunz were in one boat and Joel, Jason, and I were in an-other, and you caught that forty-two-inch northern about ten minutes after we got on the water? Remember? We all motored straight to Musky Pasture and started casting around those un-derwater boulders, and you were into that fish on your second or third cast?"

"Sure — I was off to one of the best starts of my life. After that fish was in the net, I wasn't too worried about how many I would catch the rest of the day."

"So you probably remember that after your fish we didn't really get into anything decent for hours. We picked up a hammerhandle now and then, but nothing big."

"After my big pike it was a little tough — I remember that."

"And then for our last half hour we all decided to fish around the reefs in Ament Bay. I even remember what I was throwing — a magnum silver Bomber minnow that had been chewed up quite a bit by smaller pike. There Joel and Jase and I were, sitting off that big reef south of the island, and I was cast-ing along the edges of the reef. Cast, cast, cast. And then one time, when I had pretty much assumed that nobody was going to have any action, when I had even started to wonder what we were going to have for supper that night, just when I was fin-ishing a retrieve and my Bomber was about four feet from the side of the boat — it was so close to the side of the boat that I could almost reach out and touch it — this huge pike — my goodness, Dad, its back was as thick as a corner post — this huge pike came out from under the boat and absolutely en-gulfed my Bomber — whomp, the whole minnowbait — and then rocketed completely out of the water, flipped, and dove as if it wanted to tunnel into the lakebed."

"I remember that. From where we were in our boat, we could hear this big commotion. That must have been about a week's worth of excitement right there."

"It was exciting for a few seconds. That fish dove, my drag started screaming but then caught, I was all over myself trying to get my thumb on the release so I could free spool, my rod bucked once again, and then *bwink* — I was left with a tag end of line dangling from the end of my rod as the fish flashed its side and disappeared."

"What kind of line were you using?"

"Seventeen-pound mono."

"Well, then, what could you do? At that point of your retrieve, what could you do? I'm telling you, Jon, nobody could have done any better with a strike like that than you did. If you had had more line out, that mono would've probably had enough stretch in it so that it wouldn't have snapped. At least it would've given you some time to loosen your drag or start free spooling. Or if you had reeled all the way up to your leader and had started your L-turn, almost for sure you would've been free spooling and could've let the fish take your lure and run. But a hit four feet from the boat, when your reel's still engaged, what can you do? What could anybody do? A fish like that is going to snap something every time. What happened to you would have happened to anyone."

"But the bad stuff keeps happening to me."

"I think you're overdoing the pity now. In the past handful of years, all of the rest of us have lost fish. That one day when we drove from our lodge on Eagle to Stewart Lake, Duzzer went one for six. Six fish on and only one landed! He says he still has nightmares about that big spotted musky that hit his bucktail fifteen feet from the boat, swam away with it in the corner of its mouth for six or seven feet, and then shook the hook off, all in plain sight."

"At least he had a fish on. The last time I went to Stewart, I was in a boat with T-Gunz and Mike the guide. Mike said he wasn't even going to fish that day; he was going to backtroll us along the rock shelves and just off the crowns of fallen trees and show us some water guaranteed to hold muskies. With help like that, I figured I was sure to get into a fish or two. But all day long T-Gunz was the only one with any action. At first I figured it was because of his lure — he was using a black and silver Crane minnow. So I switched and started casting an identical bait. Still nothing. Then I figured it was because he was casting ahead of me down the shoreline. So I asked him if he'd mind switching places with me for a while."

"What'd he say?"

"That was fine by him, but even after we switched and I was casting into water ahead of him — you just can't believe stuff like this — he was still the only one getting any hits. Every few minutes I heard these little grunts morphing into chuckles and turned to see T-Gunz fighting another fish. At one point he was smacking his bait on the water to try to clear a weed off it, and a musky came from under the motor and slashed at it — if that thing had gotten on the hook, I would have melted down right there. I'd been fishing for years and that was just his second summer. Plus all he was using was a medium-heavy bass rig, and I had these two great St. Croix combos. But he was the only one with any action. Two of the fish he landed were in the mid-forties. Nothing I tried worked. The whole day felt like I was under some kind of curse."

"I had an experience a lot like that one day in the U.P."

"Not likely."

"No, really. One year just after school got out, Duzzer and I took off for two days of fishing up at Les Cheneaux. Both days we trolled all around buoy number 10 out by the Middle Passage. The first day Duzzer got seven pike, and I didn't have a hit. We were both using silver Bomber minnows, and we were both letting our baits run the same distance behind the boat. The second day I got seven pike, and he didn't have a single hit. Again, same bait and same distance behind the boat. Not much either of us could do about the whole business but shrug."

"But at least you had that second day. I've never had that. And there's no way I can laugh about my fishing, especially these trips to Canada. Like I said, too much has felt like a kind of curse."

"Whoa. This is sounding mighty serious. What are you really thinking?"

"I don't want to make you worry."

"But that's what dads do. If it's something I can help with, I want to hear about it."

"Well — "

"I really mean it. What are you thinking?"

"I'm not sure I can say for sure."

"You might as well try to get it out in the open. It sounds like you're wrestling with things that go way beyond fishing. Are you starting to have thoughts that scare you or make you feel guilty?"

"Dad, I think you should stop."

"No, come on. You really should talk about it."

"Not sure I can."

"You have to. It'll be better."

"Well, maybe I can try a question."

"Sure, let me hear it."

"Well — I'm not sure how best to put it — but maybe this: Do you believe that God controls everything, every little thing, in our lives? Or not?"

"Whoa, this is serious stuff. About as serious as it gets. Let me see now. To tell you the truth, at different points in my life, I've given different answers to that question. Back through high school, I would hear in church that 'not a hair can fall from our heads without the will of our Father in heaven,' and I just accepted that God controls every little thing in our lives."

"But then you started to have doubts?"

"I started to wonder about the little stuff. And the stuff I did just for kicks. Like games and sports. Take the bowling I did as part of a young people's league during a couple of my college summers. I started out by wondering whether it was right for me to ask God to help me and my team win matches. Once I had started to wonder about that, I began asking why it was that some nights I'd clearly be out of the pocket and still get strikes and other days I'd be rolling what looked like perfect balls and would end up with practically impossible splits. If God was controlling all this, what could possibly have been his point? I started to wonder if he leaves some stuff in the realm of chance or coincidence. One day pins fall; one day they don't — who can explain it?"

"Thinking about chance would probably help me right now."

"I bet. After I first started thinking that God might let chance play a role in our lives, I had other experiences that reinforced those thoughts. When I went away to grad school, I ended up living in a dorm near a guy who had graduated from Wheaton. The Wheaton in Illinois. Once he found out I was a Calvin grad, we had lots of good talks. But sometimes he would scare me."

"How so?"

"Well, he clearly believed that nothing happened without God's will, and when bad things happened to him, he took every one of them as a sign of God's judgment. Even little things, like nicking himself while shaving, or stubbing a toe. After something like that, he would walk around and fret about what it was that God was punishing him for. I just couldn't see living like that. I couldn't take a shaving accident as a sign that I had to worry about the state of my soul. And it wasn't easy to believe in a god who would deliberatively cause all our little pains. So I kept telling myself that my position on chance in the universe was right. But the more I told myself this, the more I started to struggle with some new issues."

"Like what?"

"Well, for one thing, it was really hard to draw a line between all the different things in my life and say, 'These are the little things, and these are the big things.' Plus the older I got, the more some horrible things came into the picture. And at first they pushed me toward chance, too. But shortly after grad school, I got to know a young couple whose two-year-old girl got some kind of cancer, lympho- something or other — I don't remember the exact name. She went through medical procedures that left her almost a wraith, was declared recovered and started to regrow the finest wisps of blonde hair you ever saw, but then developed a different kind of cancer, and died within a month of that diagnosis. Actually, people said, the cancer didn't kill her; the chemo burned her up. When their little girl was sick, every look those parents gave me screamed for an answer. And what was I supposed to tell them — 'Unlucky for you; it was a coincidence, an unfortunate bit of chance, that your baby girl got sick, got better, got sick again, and then died'? No way I could tell them that. Not a lot of comfort people can find in coincidence."

"So where are you now?"

"Well, based on what I've told you about my past, you've probably guessed that I'm not perfectly settled yet, but I'm back to believing that God does in fact control everything. And I've come to accept that he works through everything in our lives for our ultimate good."

"No doubts about that?"

"Not really, but I also believe that in the time between now and our ultimate good, if we try to explain why things happen to us, we can go wrong in all sorts of ways. I think we're lousy interpreters — it's the easiest thing in the world for us to mistake our will and intentions and hopes for God's. And I think that how you've been trying to explain your recent fishing, especially the Canadian fishing, is off the mark too."

"What was I supposed to think about all those times these last few years when everybody else but me was able to catch a huge pike or musky?"

"Well, you certainly shouldn't start thinking that God's punishing you or turning his back on you or putting you under some sort of curse. You just can't know right now why this has gone on, and you can't be sure if it'll go on for even one more day. So you've just got to keep getting a line in the water. And you should probably take the pressure off our trips to Ontario. How many gorgeous spots have you not even really noticed because you were ticked you hadn't hooked a forty-inch pike or musky? There are other places where you can catch a big pike or musky, you know. Your big fish doesn't have to come from Canada."

"I know. It's just that it seems like the most likely spot."

"Well, I'd say that you should keep going to bodies of water where you know there are big dogs; then fish just as hard as you've always fished in the past."

"After these last years I'm tempted to give it up. Maybe I should get more serious about birding. Or golf. Grandpa says that in golf you never have days like the days when the fish don't bite."

"Grandpa's dad ruined fishing for him. And have you ever seen him golf when his slice is acting up? Some of his drives fly over more than one county. Giving up fishing would be a mistake. How about a little suggestion? As soon as we can after we've gotten back home, before you get into anything like a summer routine, let's take the boat out to Murray Lake. I'll have to explain to Mom why we need to go out fishing so soon after we've done it for a full week in Canada, but I think I can pull that off. You know Joel and Jason have gotten Master Angler fish out of Murray the past couple of summers, and there's probably a big one swimming around wondering why you've been ignoring it. What you've seen as a pattern could evaporate in our first fifteen minutes on Murray."

"I'll go if you want to, if you really think there's a chance it will help."

"I think there's all the chance in the world."

This might not have been the best idea I've ever had, I thought, just three days later, as I pulled up the trolling motor so that Jon and I could use the outboard to change locations on Murray Lake once again. We had already fished every spot on the lake where anyone in our family had ever seen or caught a musky. And we had tried just about every lure and tactic we knew of. But we had caught just one musky, only twenty-five inches, and I'm not sure why it had found my bucktail more attractive than Jon's nearly identical one, but the fact of the matter is that it had. As Jon had put down his rod and reached for the net, preparing to land my fish, he had refused to meet my eyes, and I, for the first time in my life, had wished that a fish had ignored my lure.

"We're not done yet," I said as we left the knuckle cove on the west side and headed for the tip of the lake's main peninsula. "We've got enough light for one more crack at a spot we tried earlier. How about we give that small bay south of the eastern launch ramp one last shot?"

"We can if you want. But I think the fish knew I was coming and decided to settle on the bottom and snooze."

"That's rubbish and you know it. We'll give that bay another shot. We've got about twenty minutes of daylight to work with yet. I think I'm going to toss my old Bull Dawg. What about you?"

"I'll probably try this Burt. In Canada last week Jason got most of his big ones with a Burt that he just twitched through the weeds. He said he had figured out how to annoy the fish into biting."

Jon's first cast was tight to shore, and a few seconds after his Burt landed, he set the hook forcefully.

"At last!" I exhaled deeply. "That's a fish, right?"

"Not sure. It felt like it at first, but now it seems to be dragging in. Aw, shoot. It's just a big weed, roots and all — probably the only forty-incher I'm ever going to catch."

"Try the other side of the boat once. In the past we've caught suspended fish out there."

"Okay, one cast on the deep side. There. Wait — Dad, Dad, I've got a hit. That's a fish. That's a fish for sure. Look at my line slicing the surface. Man, was that a hit — the fish absolutely nailed it. But now there's not all that much resistance."

"It's probably swimming straight at us."

"Naw, it's trying to angle away from us. But I don't think — no, see, it's up on the surface. It's a musky, but it's not that big, probably just nineteen or twenty inches. Just big enough to hit hard."

"Want me to get the net?"

"Naw. I can release this one by hand. Hand me those pliers, will you? There. There you go, little musky, go on home and send your mama this way."

"Where there's one fish there might be another, probably a bigger one. Try another cast out that way."

"What? You think I'm going to hook up on two casts in a row? Oh, what the world; I guess it can't hurt. One more cast into the deep water with my killer Burt."

When his Burt landed on the surface, a musky, a big broad musky this time, almost certainly close to forty inches, smashed the lure from a rear quarter, came entirely out of the water in a perfect arc, turned and did a side flop into the water, and then dove and powered toward the opposite shore.

"Now that's just plain unbelievable." Jon was shaking his head as he loosened his drag. "Maybe you better fight this fish. I don't have any experience with fish this big!"

"You're going to get some right now. Make sure your drag is

set right and trust your equipment. Just remember: Your rod and reel can handle fifty-pound muskies. The one on the end of your line right now is probably twenty-five. I'll use the trolling motor to keep us out in deep water. That fish has your name written on it."

I have seen some fights between humans and fish in my life, fights in which things went so wackily wrong that people to whom I have described those fiascoes have seemed reluctant to believe me, even though they know I am mainly a reliable story-teller. On about eight different occasions I have seen anglers shatter expensive graphite rods, leaving themselves with something like a two-foot stub of a rod with which to try to put pressure on a fish. Once a friend of mine had about a thirty-five-inch pike right up to the side of our boat when he took one hand off his rod to try to keep the sweat from running into his eyes and then was shocked when that fish dove straight down and pulled his rod and reel out of his other hand and out of sight into the lake. And below Tippy Dam once, I saw someone fishing with what looked like saltwater gear pull back so hard on a fall-run king salmon that he tore the treble hook on his spoon right out of the salmon's mouth and tore it out with so much force that it shot straight back at him and pierced the forearm that he had barely managed to put up to shield his face.

Nothing wacky happened as Jon fought his musky on Murray Lake that day. The fish made a determined run toward a guano-splattered swimming raft, but Jon managed to stop her and turn her back toward our boat. And just as I was about to net her, she started rolling on the surface, wrapping her snoot right up in the leader and line, but she didn't catch any part of the line on her gill cover, so within a couple of minutes I had her in the net and, leaving the net and fish over the side in the water, I turned everything over to Jon.

"Glory, glory, hallelujah!" I was singing without any thought about proper pitch, forgetting that there were people on decks of cottages who could hear me. "If that fish isn't a forty, I'll eat my raincoat. You had to wait, no one's ever going to argue about that, you had to wait, but God ended up giving you a special blessing. For you it's like that scene from *A River Runs through It* where the minister smiles knowingly and says something like 'God's been good to all of us this afternoon, but it looks as if he's been particularly gracious to me.'"

"I can hardly believe it. I'm going to have to sit and think this through. But first I've got to get her untangled and out of the net. Can't hurt a fish like this. Such a big female can make a lot of babies next spring. These genes need to stay in the system."

"Okay. It looks like she's got cords of the net wrapped around her mouth. Better start with that. Do you see how that cord twists and then comes around by her eye?"

"Yeah, there we go. One more strand here and I think she'll be free of the net. Stop that thrashing! Shoot! Now I've got to do some of that work over again. There we go. Okay, she's free of the net. Can you hand me the pliers?"

"Here you go. How's she hooked?"

"This is really weird. Every other fish I've ever seen hooked on a Burt has the front treble right in the corner of the mouth and the back treble either hanging loose on the outside or snagged under the throat. This one took the whole lure in, hind end first. That back treble's pretty deep. Here. Can you keep its jaws spread? I used to have a jaw-spreader, but Joel or Jason must have it. Easy, easy. Watch those teeth! Shoot — I can't quite reach that back treble from here. It looks like it's way down by the gills. I think one of those hooks might have nicked its gills."

"Want me to give it a try?"

"Maybe. I can't quite get a grip on that hook with the pliers. It's too deep."

"Let me try from under the gill cover. Sometimes if you come in from underneath, you can get a good angle. There. I see where the hook is. Just about got it. Come on now. There we go. Yeah, the hook is loose, so go ahead and try to wiggle the lure out. Easy. Easy. Got it?"

"Yup. It's out. Whew — that was a little more surgery than I'm used to in a boat."

"For me too. Here's your fish. Get a good grip on it, and I'll snap a couple of quick pictures. Got to get her back in the water. We had to work longer than usual."

After I had snapped some pictures, Jon leaned over and gently put his fish back in the lake. He held her upright in the water just ahead of the tail and began to twist her body ever so slightly.

"What do you think? How's she coming? Any tension in her muscles yet?"

"Shoot — I didn't see that before."

"What? What is it?"

"There's a line of blood threading from her gill. I don't like that. Bleeding from the gills is never a good sign."

"Just keep working her. Take your time. We're in no rush — our fishing is done for the day. Try her once. Can she stay upright without you?"

"Just as I'm about to let her go, I can feel her trying to stay upright, but then she starts to go over on her side."

"No pulling away from you?"

"Not really."

"Work her a little more and then give her another try on her own."

"This fish is gonna die, Dad."

"You don't know that for sure. Give her some more of those gentle twists."

"Naw, Dad, I know a fish that's not going to make it when I see it. No way this fish is gonna live."

"Well, now, don't start. Don't even think about starting. If you're going to fish, stuff like this happens. Sometimes they get hooked in the lip, and sometimes they take hooks deep. This fish did it to herself. Who ever heard of a fish taking a whole Burt straight down the throat? So you don't have to give me that look. It's not your fault. You got that? It's not your fault. This kind of stuff can happen to anyone. It's happened to me plenty of times, with all kinds of fish. If you want to call it something, call it an accident, a freak accident."

Jon didn't respond. He was still holding his fish by the tail, but he had stopped giving its body little twists.

"What?" My throat muscles were tightening up. "What? What are you thinking? Just say something. Jon? What's going on? Come on, you've got to talk."

"Do you remember when you told me you think we're all lousy interpreters?"

"Yeah, sure. What about it?"

"Well, one minute this is all a special blessing from God — glory, hallelujah, and all that. And then the next minute it's a freak accident. Since when can we have things both ways?"

Two Are Better Than One

I t wasn't surprising, really, that our friends were concerned about how Wanda and I would cope with what they called an "empty nest." After all, they knew that even as our three sons grew into their late teens, they didn't act as many of their peers did, wanting to have nothing to do with their parents apart from asking for and accepting their financial support. In fact, our sons continued to enjoy with us the kinds of things that we as a family had enjoyed together for years.

If Wanda and I mentioned that we felt like taking a ride out to the general store in Smyrna, which for years served a single-scoop ice cream cone that clearly deserved a spot in Ripley's as among the largest in the world, Jon, Joel, and Jason would beat us into the car. If I said on a fall Sunday afternoon that I felt like driving up to Croton Pond to check how much orange and yellow the maples and aspens were throwing onto the pond's surface, the boys would grab their cameras and come along. Even when Wanda and I said we felt like heading out to Fallasburg Park to set up folding chairs on the river's edge and read for a while, the boys would ask us to wait for them to pack some fishing equipment so that they could wade the river and try to catch some smallmouth.

So it made sense for our friends to be concerned about Wanda and me. And as a matter of fact, I too was somewhat worried about what life would be like once the boys left our house. But only somewhat. What I was more deeply worried about was what fishing trips would be like once one or more of them left my boat. Not just occasionally, which was inevitable. But for good.

For the times I had spent with them in the boat had provided the kinds of memories I never wanted to stop making. The four of us had made some truly impressive catches. One day on Miner Lake, we caught ninety-six largemouth bass, most of them over sixteen inches long. One rainy afternoon on Muskegon Lake, we landed nearly forty heavy-shouldered northern pike. And in less than two hours on a mucky point in a channel in the Les Cheneaux Islands, we caught and then very carefully unhooked over 150 bullheads.

And our impressive catches extended to creatures other than fish. Several times we had seagulls dive-bombing and then flying off a bit with one of our floating minnowbaits. More than once we caught slime-coated and extremely irritated snapping turtles. And on one scary and potentially dangerous occasion, we hooked a deep-feeding cormorant.

You can see, I'm sure, why I hoped such adventures would go on and on. And you might guess that if my hopes were to be threatened, they would be threatened first by the leave-taking of Jon, our oldest. And your guess would be right.

It happened when he was in his early twenties. "How about tomorrow for a trip to Muskegon Lake?" I asked the three boys.

Joel and Jason were ready to start loading the van a day early. But then Jon rocked things by saying "Can't — got other plans for tomorrow."

And what did those and related plans often involve? Birds. He had become a birder. I didn't know exactly how and when it had happened. To this day Jon himself insists that he doesn't know exactly how and when it had happened. But it had happened.

When he and I were riding in the van, he would often ask me to pull over and stop — sometimes alongside fairly busy roads — so that he could get out and try to capture a picture of a kestrel or merlin perched on a utility pole. More than once he suggested that it would be far more stewardly and rewarding for me to use waders not to pursue smallmouth bass in local rivers but to seek prothonotary warblers in nearby swamps. And instead of asking me to take him to Muskegon Lake or the Muskegon River, he started bugging me about trips to the Muskegon Wastewater Facility with its enormous waterfowl-attracting lagoons.

But the birding wasn't all. Often he would be away from home for extended periods of time. When Wanda and I dared to ask about his whereabouts and he decided to answer, he said only that he had been at a friend's house. At a later point, he started getting phone calls at home, checking the number, and then hustling out of the house to carry on a conversation while seated on our front porch or walking up and down our street. After that, he gave himself away when he accidentally came back into the house before signing off and referred to the person on the line as "Babe."

Wanda and I realized he had a girlfriend. Once we had figured this out, things started to happen almost more quickly than we could absorb. Wanda and I met the "Babe," otherwise known as Tiffany. We treated the young couple to several Sunday dinners. We started having to signal our descent into our basement, where the couple would watch movies in the near-dark, with various kinds of noises. We four had extremely competitive games of Rook on various weekend evenings, always following Tiffany's (Kansas) rules about where the Rook fit into the power structure of the game. Jon started spending more time at Tiffany's house than he did at ours. The pronoun *we* assumed a more and more prominent place in Jon's talk. Jon planned an excursion for Tiff and himself to Ludington State Park. There the two of them took a hike past the lighthouse. Tiff returned from that walk displaying a diamond ring on her hand. When they got home, they stopped over to give us time to make appreciative noises about the ring. Wanda and I received directions for various errands preparatory to the wedding. And then in early May, we all put on the formal clothes we had bought or rented and then drove out to Post Family Farms in Hudsonville for a formal wedding ceremony and not-so-formal reception. During and after this time, it was clear to everyone that Jon and Tiff were almost cross-eyed with love for each other. And I, who had come to see the world in terms — perhaps fairly stereotypical terms — of what a father could do with sons, found that for the first time in my life I had a daughter.

When Jon and Tiff returned from their honeymoon, I realized that my fears of never again having Jon in my boat could well be realized. It was pretty clear to me (I was relearning things about young love) that he would not participate in a recreational activity for any extended period of time without her. Still, that was not an insurmountable problem. I knew that Tiff had fished in her youth, for she had told us stories of fishing for catfish in reservoirs in Kansas with the person she called her "Grandpaw." More serious was the fact that she and Jon were on an exceedingly tight budget. They had attended a series of seminars featuring Dave Ramsey tapes, and they had decided that his suggestion of allotting themselves a certain amount of cash each month to use as "fun money" was a sterling idea. But the amount of their fun money was so startlingly small that I worried I would never be able to talk the two of them into buying Michigan fishing licenses. And for reasons I have never been able to understand fully, they were reluctant to accept charity from me.

Fortunately, by the time they had gotten somewhat settled in their home, it was early June, and each year toward the middle of June the state of Michigan offers a free fishing weekend. Once I remembered this, I called and invited them to come with Wanda and me for an evening of fishing. And I sweetened the offer with the promise of dinner not at some fast-food joint but at a sit-down restaurant like the Bostwick Lake Inn. I knew a little about the kinds of dinners their Ramsey-strict budget was forcing on them, so my offer, I felt confident, was one they simply could not refuse.

"What do you think we should fish with?" Jon had started to arrange gear in the back of the boat as soon as I had cut the engine in three or four feet of water on the far east side of Wabasis Lake.

"Brown tubes. I can rig everybody up. You and Tiff can fish

off the back. Wanda, how about moving your folding chair up here next to me?"

"Sounds good. You can unhook all the fish I catch."

"And I'm sure you'll keep me busy. So once I've got everybody rigged up, look for patches of sand or light gravel, pitch a tube on them, give the tube little jerks or hops, and if you feel any resistance at all, set the hook."

"Flipping tubes, eh?" Jon looked skeptical. "That's a pretty subtle technique. Don't forget that I haven't fished seriously in quite a while. And Mom and Tiff have probably never used a tube. You don't want to turn us all off to fishing in one night, do you?"

"I didn't get all this gray hair by being stupid."

"So you always say."

"And I mean it. Just wait; this is all going to work out. I've brought the Bass Pro rods you and Mom always used in the past. And I've got a brand new St. Croix rod for Tiff. Super sensitive. She'll be able to feel a minnow nibbling her bait. Plus I fished this stretch of water just the day before yesterday, and all I threw was brown tubes. They were magic. Something's drawing crayfish to these sandy patches, and the bass are in here gorging on them. Every bass I caught came into the boat barfing up crayfish bits. And brown tubes look almost exactly like crayfish. So we'll get into some fish. Here you go, Tiff; you're all set up."

"Thanks. This is guaranteed to catch fish for me at some point in my lifetime?"

"No, no, no. It's guaranteed to catch fish for you *tonight*."

Tiff took the rod and, after a few additional notes of instruction from Jon, pitched the tube ten or twelve feet from the boat.

Then she engaged the reel and jigged the tube off the bottom gently; as she did so, we all could see a medium-sized bass approach from the side, take the bait in, shoot to the surface, tailwalk away from us, and toss the bait.

"See," I gloated, "our very first cast. A little harder snap of the rod tip next time, okay, Tiff?"

"Gotcha. That one kinda surprised me. I'll land the next one." She had a look of extreme determination on her face.

"No harm done. There's more where that one came from. I can see it already — we're gonna catch a mess of bass."

I like it when I'm right. And that night I was. As soon as I had Wanda and myself rigged up, we joined Tiff in fighting a bass every two or three casts.

And Jon? After he insisted on rigging his own rod up, he did as he often did in the boat as a kid. He leaned his rod against one of the gunnels. Then he dug his binoculars out of his rucksack and started scanning the shoreline.

"What's the deal?" I swiveled in my seat to get his attention. "Afraid you've lost your touch with the fishies?"

"No way. It's just that local birders have reported a red-headed woodpecker working around the lake here. Plus there's supposed to be an eagles' nest up around Wabasis Avenue and Twelve Mile, and the adults have been spotted flying across the lake. A red-headed and a bald would be firsts for me this year. Plus I hope you didn't forget that I don't have to fish all the time to catch the beasts. All those trips when I was young I would take my breaks and still end up catching bigger fish than you did."

"Whoa! That's a challenge if I've ever heard one. If you're sitting there practically exploding with skill, why don't you pick up your rod and we'll see whether it's you or me catching the big fish in the next few minutes. Loser buys ice cream on the way home. You up for that?"

"Can't you hear my knees knocking? You know I can take you in a fishing contest any day, any lake."

"Okay, big talker. You fish off the back, and I'll fish up here. Equally good territory in both places, right?"

"Probably. Doesn't make a lot of difference to me."

"Okay, so here we go. The big fish in the next few minutes wins."

I swiveled back toward the front and scanned the water to my left and right. There, I thought — a large spread of sand that looked identical to those that had been producing all evening and that had so far not been touched.

"Let me have this one, okay?" Only Wanda could hear me.

"Sure, but try not to let this father-son competition get too serious."

"When do we ever do that?"

"Yeah, right." She made a little pooh-pooh sound.

Taking care not to hook her on my backcast, I sent my tube to the far side of the sandy stretch. Then I let it sit for a few seconds. As we drifted, I dragged it, stirring up a little cloud of sand. Then I gave it a couple of pronounced hops and let it sit again. I focused on the line as it entered the water. *Yes, yes, yes — there it was, I thought, the most subtle of twitches. But it absolutely was a twitch. A little more and I'm gonna let you have it.*

Just then, though, my concentration was cut into by a sharp "ungh" from the back of the boat. It sounded more like Tiff than Jon, and it was followed by some rocking commotion in the boat and some splashing in the water, but I didn't have time to turn and check what was going on since I now could feel pronounced jerks on my own line.

I reared back and set the hook, immediately feeling the throbbing resistance of desperate life on the other end. The fish stayed down and took drag as it pulled away from me. *All the really good ones stay down,* I exulted to myself. But then I sucked air sharply as the fish turned and headed straight back toward me, nearly putting a loop of slack in the line. *Reel!* I told myself. And I did, rapping my knuckles on the body of the reel as I neared panic mode. As the fish approached the boat, it stayed down, pulled its way under the keel, and then tried to turn toward the bow, where it could wrap the line around the trolling motor. "No, no, no," I didn't even try to keep my voice down; "I'm bringing you back this way." So I stuck my rod tip deep in the water, pointed it away from the fish's path, and worked that beast past the keel and into the open water on the side of the boat, where Wanda had the net ready and waiting. As soon as the fish was in the net and the line went slack, the tube fell out of the corner of its mouth.

"It's yours," Wanda laughed, "but just barely."

"It should be mine," I answered; "the Lord loves a righteous angler." I reached into the net, got the bass, all eighteen or nineteen inches of it, by its lower lip, held it up, and then turned to face Jon and Tiff.

"Behold!" I knew how to be smug.

"No, you behold!" Jon shot back. He and Tiff were standing side by side, she with her arm around his back. In his raised right hand was another bass, a bass easily three or four inches longer than mine.

I slipped my fish back into the water and waited for it to get its bearings and then swim off. "Okay, Jon," I conceded, "that's a great fish. In fact, it's probably the biggest fish I've seen out of this lake in the last three or four years. So I buy the ice cream. I don't mind losing to a fish like that."

"Well, that's good," Jon's smile was quirky. "And that's progress, too, since it seems you've learned how to be a more gracious loser since the last time I fished with you and you started one of these hopeless little contests."

"Maybe I've learned a thing or two. An old guy can still learn, can't he? But hold on a second — I've got a question for you."

"What's that?"

"When did you start using the St. Croix rod?"

Time in a Bottle

Boat-launch sites aren't the only places it happens, but they are where it happens most often. I don't have to be on my own to feel it, but that is when it hits me the hardest. There's really not much difference: I can be preparing to launch my boat, trying to control the adrenaline-stoked hope for a great catch, or centering the boat on the trailer after some time on the water, relishing the memory of a recent release. But at some point I see a child, usually a boy around five years old, playing in or around a boat under the mostly watchful eye of an adult. And I feel a deep, pulsing pang.

It happened most recently just last week. As I prepared to launch at Murray Lake, I noticed that poking around in a boat nosed up on the shore to the side of the launch-ramp dock was a little buzz-cut blondie who was trying to help the man I took to be his dad sort out gear before they shoved off and started to fish.

After I launched my boat, tied it up to the dock, parked my van, and then walked back to the boat, I decided to sit in it where it was and take care of some pre-fishing errands. No one was waiting to launch behind me. And I needed to sharpen some hooks and check some knots. Plus part of me wanted to keep an ear on the little guy and his dad, only ten or twelve yards away from me.

As I worked and listened, I couldn't fight off the thought that the pang must be connected to something that in large measure I have lost and desperately want to regain. But exploring that thought got me started on a fairly stern self-lecture: *Be serious. What deep part of your brain, what part not fully under rational control, would ever suggest that you trade your current days on the water, however infrequent they might be, with your strong and skilled sons, now all twenty-something years old, for the days when they were just little guys in the earliest stages of learning to fish? Really now, a logical look at things should show that there's no comparison between what it was like to fish with them then and what it's like to fish with them now.*

When Jon, Joel, and Jason were young, the pressure on me to put them on fish almost immediately after we got on the water was intense. In those days, "They're not biting, Dad" was close to the most threatening sentence I ever heard from them. After only five or ten minutes of casting with no hits, one of them would usually start rummaging in his pee-wee tackle box for a new lure. When the five or ten minutes stretched to fifteen or twenty, they would put down their rods and start digging into our cooler of snacks for the day. And when we reached thirty minutes without any bites, they would announce that they wanted to move.

"Boys," I would say, unable to conceal my sigh, "we've barely begun to fish this spot — we can't pull up so soon and start flying all over the lake."

"Why not?" they would counter. "No fish around here. We've gotta move."

But after I did move, and we had spent fifteen or twenty minutes in a new spot, again with no action, they wanted to move again.

"Come on, fish, start to bite," I would mutter under my breath, because I knew that after about an hour of no luck, my sons would want me to take them back to the launch site. There we would lug all of our fishing equipment from the boat to the van and then load the boat anew, this time with tubing equipment. That I would then spend the rest of the day towing one or two of them at a time around the lake on our tube seemed almost profane. And sometimes when we stopped to let them crawl back on the tube after a flip, I would notice the bold icons of big fish on my fish finder.

Now that my sons are grown, it seems as if we've been transported to another world to fish. No more do I have to fear their impatience, their clamoring to roar from place to place, their readiness to abandon fishing gear altogether. It seems easy for them to stand alertly in a boat on a musky hunt for eight or nine hours a day. And no longer do they think about new spot after new spot; they find a promising and well-defined area and then seek out and focus on what they call "the spot on the spot." When they were young, we used to fish our way along lengthy drop-offs fairly quickly. Now they find the one spot along that drop-off where a small subsurface peninsula holds a clump of cabbage, and they start their dissecting. Or they find the place where a line of boulders stops but points the way along an underwater saddle to a cluster of rocks in deeper water. They fish spots like these at different depths, from different angles, and with different kinds of baits. When they are finished with such spots, every square foot of them has had some kind of lure pass within inches.

Their patience is almost inexhaustible. More than once I've seen them go for a couple of full days without landing a musky. If they get a musky to follow, that's good. If they get a musky to go around once or more on the figure eight, perhaps nipping at the flashabou on their spinner, that's better. They assure me that once they know where a big fish lives, they'll return periodically until they get it to hit. When they fish, they are young men of unshakeable hope, hope that sooner or later — there is always the next cast — a musky will rise and engulf their lure.

Describing their patience on the water reminds me of how far they've come in casting ability. When they were young — my goodness, often they were frantic, they were wild, they were dangerous.

Their equipment then was certainly not very good. At the start they used four- or five-foot fiberglass rods with closed-face reels with Disney characters printed on them.

And they seemed to pay no attention to where they were casting. How far they could sling baits — that was what was important. So quite often they would whip their rod behind them in frenetic loops, they would get their line wrapped around their rod tip, they would then shift from backcast to violent cast, their line would snap, and then their lures would go flying off to land where we didn't dare to retrieve them — usually on people's beaches or lakeside decks. If their line didn't get wrapped and then snap, then they often cast their lures into all sorts of snags — stumps, weeping-willow branches, parts of docked boats, swimming rafts, and once altogether too close to a golden retriever that had launched itself from a dock and swum halfway out to us in the boat before being frantically called back to shore.

"Hey, hey, hey!" I would chide.

"Hey, hey, hey what?" they would cackle back. "You can't be afraid to go where the big fish are." To them this meant as close to objects as possible, and I had to admit that "as close as possible" to these objects was smart. On, over, or wrapped around them was foolish.

The worst part of their wildness came when they paid little or no attention to their backcasts and then embedded their hooks where they weren't welcome. Once Jason took Jon's favorite Little League cap off his head and into a very shallow mucky cove that I didn't dare take the boat into. And once Joel sank two of the three hooks of a lure into Jason's right triceps. Within minutes Jason began sinking into shock, so our vastly abbreviated day on the water taught us little about angling and much about how to find a hospital emergency room and then not be ignored there.

Now that the boys are grown, the equipment they use is heavy enough to handle many saltwater species. They use medium- and heavy-action rods eight and one-half to nine feet long. These allow them to throw baits that can be as long as eighteen inches and weigh as much as a pound. It's hard to get all four of us together at one time anymore, but occasionally we're able to get three of us together in the boat — two sons in the front and me in the back. When two of them fish side by side, it's like a waltz on water. Their casting accuracy is amazing. When they cast toward objects that I was almost paranoid about in my harping to them as kids — like the gas lines of moored pontoons — they land their baits six inches short. When they cast toward things that I had been somewhat less worried about in our early years — like the chains holding offshore swimming rafts in place — they land their baits three inches short. And when they cast toward objects that I apparently never said anything about — like buoys marking a slalom ski course — they usually smack their baits right off the objects' near sides.

No one ever loses or breaks a lure; no one ever hooks anyone else. And their casting and retrieving is synchronized. As one brings his bait to boatside and starts his figure eight, the other's bait is landing in the water about twenty-five yards out. Thus they ensure that a following musky sees only one lure at a time and doesn't get confused or spooked as the fish nears the boat. All in all, as they work a spot over, they are models of robotic precision.

So as I sat in my docked boat at Murray and finished retying a couple of knots, I concluded that, when it came to my fishing companions at least, there was no way imaginable that my sons as little guys would have any advantage over my sons as grown men.

So why, I wondered, do I feel the loss? How about some rational control? Let's get it straight, Vande Kopple.

And then words from the nearby boat cut through all memory, cut through all interpretation, and cut, in fact, straight to the deepest of my deep places:

"Look, Dad, my line's all tangled."

"Nathan! That's a mess. What did you do?"

"I didn't do a thing. Really, Dad — it just happened."

"Hey, bud, let me tell you something you should already know — things like that don't just happen."

"Sometimes they do. They really do. You know they do. But you can fix it, right, Dad?"

The Old Man in the Lee

A few weeks ago I saw the following report on the internet message board of the Michigan Muskie Alliance. It was posted by a member who, like me, lives in Grand Rapids:

> July 18   Murray Lake   6-9:30 p.m.
> *Water temperature: 77 degrees, visibility: 8-10 feet, weed growth: normal Fished from just after supper until dusk. Moved six fish total — four lazy follows, one that ate but spit the hook on its second jump, one (43") that hit the net. A good night on the water.*

The first post in response was from my youngest son, Jason, who is vigilant in reading fishing reports from Alliance members:

> *Also on Murray last night. With the old man. Netted three fish, including the old man's personal best (47"). Awesome night on the water!*

The information in the first post about water temperature, visibility, and amount of weed growth seemed right to me. And Jason certainly had not messed up with the count of fish in our net or with the length of the spotted beauty that was my new personal best.

But what was the deal with the reference to his "old man"? I knew that some young guys referred to their fathers this way. But why would it occur to Jason to use that name over all other possibilities for me? Could this son — could all of my sons — actually think of me as an old guy? I was shocked to consider it.

Certainly I showed some signs of age. After all, how could anyone make it to sixty without some slowing down, some tightening up, some wearing out?

But I probably showed fewer such signs than most people my age. And I certainly didn't think of myself as falling-apart old. In fact, a rather robust part of my consciousness still wanted to believe I was eighteen or nineteen, driving the circuit at Holland State Park on Sunday nights trying to attract attention from what my friends and I called "wild things." Had I slipped, and slipped without even being aware of it? It bothered me to suspect that maybe that's how slips work.

The more I gnawed at this question, the more I recalled scattered bits of ribbing and kidding my sons had tossed my way the past few years while we were together in the boat. Were these actually lighthearted jokes among fishing equals to help pass the time when we couldn't get fish to strike? Or did they add up to something? Might my boys already be embarrassed in some way by what I could not do? Might they see me as someone who needed special help from them on fishing excursions? Might I someday actually become a kind of burden in the boat so that they would secretly prefer to leave me behind on shore?

A few days after the night of my personal best, Wanda and I were looking through one of the first memory books she had ever made, one celebrating Jason as a young angler. One picture stood out in the way the flint-like surface of the water in the frame was set off by Wanda's chosen background of navy. There Jason and I were (Jon or Joel must have taken the picture), in shallow water framed by partially undercut cedars along the shore of the Muskegon River. I had my left hand on Jason's shoulder, and with my right I was pointing out across the water to something, probably a spawning bed, that Jason apparently hadn't seen. My guess is that I was probably also indicating to him where he should cast his yarn ball so that it could float at natural current speed toward what was likely an impressive female king salmon on the bed or several males jockeying behind her.

That picture was probably taken in 1994 or 1995. Finding it easy, maybe even natural, to continue wrestling with the issue of whether my sons saw me as having begun to slide toward a nursing home, I started to recall incidents in which it was clear that Jason's vision was much sharper than mine. I had to admit that my eyesight had not grown stronger over the years. Since I was a child, I had to cope with the effects of astigmatism (bullies at school called me "Billy Four Eyes"), and although my eyes had held steady for much of my thirties and forties, it was undeniable lately that every two years or so I needed a stronger prescription. Plus the peripheral vision I had once taken so much pride in while playing basketball and volleyball also seemed to be narrowing.

The vision I am working with at sixty years of age leaves me missing some of the muskies that follow my lure to boatside, especially those that come in low and late.

"Dad," Jason will hiss, "you've got a follow! There, there, right there!"

"Huh? Where?" I frantically scan the water and still see nothing.

Jason likes to tell the story about how once I was reeling a bucktail in close to the boat when he spotted a low follow, he yelled to me to keep the lure going, I did an L-turn with my lure and sped it up as I swung it to the outside, and I ended up catching a forty-three-inch musky without ever seeing the fish until I set the hook and the fish exploded from the water with one of my treble hooks in its snoot.

Another challenge for me is that I have developed floaters in my left eye. When they first appeared, I thought I had suffered a detached retina. But, no, my optometrist said, your retina is fine; you've just got a couple of floaters. It happens to people our age (he looked much older than I). He seemed unimpressed that I could describe their shape very precisely: one looked like a longer-than-average inverted comma; the other looked like a pair of headphones. He thought they would disappear eventually. He obviously took a very long view of *eventually*, since months later those floaters are still with me. And they bother me more in fishing than he thought they would, since even when I'm paying what I think is excellent attention to my lure and what might be following it, those floaters can suddenly appear from the left in my field of view and startle me, sometimes so much that I stop my retrieve. Then I brace myself, for I know that whichever son is with me that day is sure to make some wisecrack like, "Dad, Dad, that's an old guy's lazy retrieve. You've got to keep the bait moving. Stop it like that and the fish is gone."

When Wanda turned a later page in her book, I inhaled sharply enough that I startled her. Another picture of me and Jason, this one more dramatic than the other. I had no memory of who might have taken the shot. I wasn't even sure where it had been taken, probably somewhere up north. But there the two of us were, I grasping a fly rod in my right hand, he and I linked, my left hand to his right, he holding a smallish fly rod in his left hand. And we're at least three feet in the air above a little brook-trout creek, apparently confident of a soft and secure landing between scrubby alder bushes. The photo was dated on the back: 1997.

No matter how hard I resist, I have to admit that I can't make jumps like that anymore. About four years ago, without any notice whatsoever, while I was simply walking to my office after a class, I felt a sharp, pulling pain in my left hip. It'll pass, I thought. But it didn't. In fact, in subsequent days it got so bad that I couldn't even teach a fifty-minute class without trying to find ways every so often to sit on a desk and throw out a discussion question, appropriate at the time or not. Parties during which I was supposed to stand and talk with various groups of people for an hour or so made me feel as if I had given the wrong answer in the Inquisition.

So I sought advice from some colleagues in physical education and learned that I might have strained or torn a hip flexor. After a few visits to a physical therapist, during which he tried to do things with my body that I'm certain it was never intended to do, things that ended up doing my hip no good whatsoever, I went to my primary-care physician, had an x-ray taken, and got the following news: "It's bone on bone. No cartilage at all. Time for a hip replacement. I'll refer you to my favorite orthopedic surgeon. He's my brother-in-law."

My new titanium hip is supposed to be stronger than the bone I grew up with. But it didn't come without some lasting trouble. For one thing, during preparation for my surgery, I heard so often about what could displace a surgically implanted hip that I became rather paranoid. The pain of a displacement, all the nurses said, would be excruciating. Never cross your left leg over your right! Don't plant your feet and twist! Don't move your toes way out to the side and then put weight on your foot!

So although physically my hip is supposed to be strong and secure, I don't fully trust it. Ask me to attempt another jump with Jason like the one caught on film and I'll find an excuse. I'm afraid I'll land and pop the titanium bulb right out of its socket and then out of my skin. It would be a shame, but I would have to choose a sloshy wade or a long detour in place of an exuberant leap.

The other bit of trouble after my surgery involves pain in my lower back opposite of the surgically repaired hip. Before surgery I never had such knots in my lower right side. Maybe one leg is now longer than the other. Or longer than it used to be and my back doesn't like the change. It feels as if someone inserted a rod into my back, stitched muscles from all sides to that rod, and then twisted the rod until the muscles were just on the edge of tearing. Maybe past the edge.

It will probably not surprise you to know that I'm most likely to develop these aching knots when I'm standing in the boat while musky fishing. Stand, cast, retrieve, watch closely, do the figure eight, then repeat, time after time after time. My boys can do this all day long. I need a little break every thirty minutes or so to try to get my back to unknot. But if I take a break, the ribbing starts: "Dad, are you falling apart? You know you can't sit down and musky fish. Either stand up and pay attention or you might as well take a nap. Just don't fall asleep on part of the net."

One page over from the one with the picture of us two leaping fly fishermen, Wanda had inserted a picture of me and all three of our boys. I immediately recognized the location: We were in Potagannissing Bay on Drummond Island. We were in a rented aluminum boat. I was in the stern, running the motor. Jon and Joel were on the seat immediately in front of me, one trolling with a rod held out to the far side of the boat, the other trolling with a rod held out to the near side. Jason was in the front seat, and he was holding up toward the camera one of the boat's bright yellow cushions on which appeared the word HELP! in bold black letters.

He might have been playing a joke, having a little fun with his mother on shore, who had to have been the one taking the picture. But he might have been somewhat serious and a little scared, because that time, I remember, I had decided to go trolling in seas fairly heavy for such a small boat. In the picture you can see spray from the bow being whipped toward us in the back.

It was an unusually windy day, and maybe I should have waited until after supper, when the wind usually calmed down, but we had driven five hours to Drummond Island, I figured, and we didn't have long to stay on the island. So, I thought, *we should get some fishing in while we can.* The boys were young and not very excited about going out, but I persuaded them. "Wind like this really oxygenates the water," I stressed. "And it stirs up baitfish all over the place — if we find schools of them, we'll find the big predators we're after. Plus, trolling into big waves will be a true adventure — like in that movie about a huge storm at sea — what's its name again? That was about eighteen years ago.

I don't talk that way very much anymore. To be perfectly honest, I have to admit that bouncing in boats in heavy waves, especially if the waves are broadside to the boat, is not my greatest pleasure. Over the years, my tailbone has taken more than enough banging; my kidneys are probably floating around inside of me. The spray from waves, running coldly down my neck and spotting my glasses, is at least annoying and sometimes on the edge of dangerous. And trying to stand up and make accurate casts is challenging because my sense of balance is not what it used to be; rock the boat just right at times and I'm having thoughts of what to try to grab onto if I start heading over the side. Plus once I'm out of the boat, in a bunk in a cabin and trying to get to sleep, I can still feel as if I'm rocking and rolling.

None of this is an issue, really, when Duzzer and I fish together, since he's even more leery of fishing in wind and waves than I am. His favorite fishing when he was young was with surface lures for bass on dead-calm nights. And his body can stand no more wave-banging than mine can. So when he and my sons and I travel to Eagle Lake on a musky hunt, he and I often choose to be in a boat together, and no matter which one of us is running the motor and selecting the spots to fish, we usually end up in similar places — around a point, in a cove, deep in the back of a bay, where the water is flat and the only sounds we hear come from terns warning us to keep our distance.

If my boys happen to see us tucked into such places, they will either motor over to chide us or chide us at greater length later, when we're all back in the cabin: "Every fish we've raised this week has come from the wind-blown side of rocks and reefs and points. The wind is pushing baitfish right onto big-fish dinner plates. If you guys want to sit and talk about your high-school girlfriends, or if you need a good place to pee, then that's all right — just go ahead and stay in the calm. But if you want to have any chance at a musky or two, you've got to get out in the wild stuff with us."

We usually don't choose to follow them. So maybe I have been fooling myself. Maybe I should just admit it. Maybe I'm showing more age than I thought. Maybe I'm on the slope, and maybe it is in fact slippery. Maybe it won't be long before my boys will actually prefer to return to a cabin and tell me stories about their fishing than have me along, perhaps only getting in their way.

Just last night I read another fishing report on the board of the Michigan Muskie Alliance. The president of the alliance was reporting on an outing to the lake within Sleepy Hollow State Park:

August 26   Lake Ovid   5-8 p.m.
Water temperature: 74 degrees, visibility: 2-3 feet, weed growth: at maximum
Had a few hours to fish with the old man. Went four for five, with the biggest one spitting the hook at boatside. Even with one lost fish, it was great to spend time together.

Not surprisingly, Jason was again the first to respond:

> Four for five is fantastic. Congrats! You can get that big one next time. Agree about the time together. Any time I get to spend with my old man in a boat is the best time of all.

I sometimes tell students that "I am a rock. I am an island. And a rock feels no pain; and an island never cries." They usually smirk, because they suspect I'm just feeding them a big line. I guess that they are smarter than I acknowledge to them, since when I saw what Jason wrote on that board, I, expecting to learn details about musky fishing and not being quite prepared to read anything about personal relationships, I, well, I, yes — there's really no point in hiding it — I wept.

PART FOUR

New to the Family

Henie's Prayer

"I worry whether she can control herself for such a long time." Wanda looked up from work on a memory book for one of her graduating students.

"What do you mean? Who's she? How long of a time?" I felt as if I had just stepped out of an elevator and into an established conversation.

"Henie. I mean Henie. Her brother is getting married Friday night, and her parents asked if I could watch her. Pick her up at two and do stuff with her until the reception in Grand Haven is finished. Could be close to midnight by the time all the celebrating's finished."

"Okay, I get it now, but what's the worry? I always thought the two of you loved spending time together."

"We do, but the last couple of years have been really rough on her, and now she can get unbelievably anxious. And since the wedding means she's losing her last sibling at home, she might be really tense. The last time she was here — a couple of weeks ago, I think — there was no big stressor that I knew about, but she started getting nervous almost as soon as she walked up the driveway."

"I guess I haven't seen so much of that. Course I'm not around her nearly as much as you are. How can you tell when she's so nervous?"

"It can get scary. She starts by asking all sorts of questions. Sometimes they're pretty much unrelated to one another. Questions, questions, questions, and she doesn't even seem to care about the answers. Then she folds her arms across her stomach and kind of caves in on herself — it's like she's trying to fold up and disappear."

"But that doesn't sound all that scary to me."

"The really scary stuff comes next. When she gets worse, she starts bringing her hands and wrists to her mouth, brushing and tapping them against her teeth. Then she starts to bite. She brings the back of a hand to her mouth, clamps down on her flesh with her front teeth, and starts to tear bits of her hand off. She's got so much scar tissue there it's not the easiest thing for her, but she always finds fresh flesh and just rips it off. It's awful — all that blood around the scar tissue on her hand and the ripped flesh between her teeth. And once or twice she's gotten this glazed look in her eyes and has come at me. Usually she goes for the side or back of my upper arm, around the triceps. If I weren't paying attention, she could probably take a pretty good chunk out of me."

"Yikes. I get it now. So her folks asked you to watch her on Friday for ten or twelve hours. What did you tell them?"

"I said I would give it a try. But I'm worried."

"Well, maybe I can think of a way to help out a little."

Henie had been one of Wanda's special-needs high-school students about twelve years earlier. Wanda had taught Henie individually for a few classes a day and also sat with her in the classes the special-education director thought Henie could handle being mainstreamed in. Through those various activities, Henie and Wanda had grown quite close. So close, in fact, that since those high-school days, Henie had asked to visit Wanda at home, in the beginning about once a week and recently less frequently.

My sons and I would usually see Henie as her mom helped her up our rather high side step and into the kitchen. And Henie would usually linger for a few minutes there with whoever happened to be around. Most of her time at our house, however, she spent downstairs with Wanda, helping to pick out pictures for memory books and occasionally pitching in as best she could with household errands. She loved feeling useful.

From what I learned about Henie's history from her mom and dad, the trouble for her started during her drawn-out birth. Her mom told me that while she was in labor with Henie, the doctor never once stopped in to check on her. And while the contractions were becoming more and more intense, a monitor started to indicate that the baby was in distress. The attending nurse dismissed those signals, though, and told Henie's mom that that monitor had been acting up a lot lately. So the nurse did nothing. The result was that Henie might well have been born healthy and bright and gorgeous like her brothers and sister, whom she still resembled in some ways, but instead had to fight through hours of pre-birth distress and was deprived of oxygen for an undetermined but significant period of time, leaving her not at all like her brothers and sister. She developed cerebral palsy, and that was associated with various kinds of dysarthria.

By the time I got to know Henie, the physical effects of her ailments were easy to see. She needed help from her mom to get out of her folks' Suburban in our driveway, and then she would try to walk on her own to our side door, rocking precariously from side to side, holding her right arm folded in over her chest, her left arm out to her side in an L with her hand twisted down and back, as if all the muscles in her forearm had cramped and constricted.

She couldn't drink anything without using a large straw; even with such a straw she had trouble keeping liquid in her mouth and would drool down her chin and onto her chest. She had a hard time bringing food directly to her mouth; she would raise a shaky hand toward her face and then, as the food got close, make an awkward lunge for it with her mouth, but she often missed and smeared her chin and cheeks with food and the associated juices. Going on thirty years old, she ate almost exactly like a nine-month-old would.

She loved to talk and tried to talk often, but in our family only Wanda could come close to understanding her consistently. Henie drew words out, and her pitch would waver, so when I talked with her, I usually ended up agreeing with almost everything she said. Her cognitive abilities were quite sound, however, so she would often have to indicate through Wanda that my "yes" didn't work in response to her questions about, say, when I had worked out during the day.

When Henie was a baby, some of her doctors had told her parents that, yes, her cognition would not be affected as drastically and negatively as many of her physical abilities. Her parents quite naturally took that as very good news, but the doctors added that as people with severe physical limitations grow into adolescence and adulthood, they and their relatives don't always find healthy cognition an unmixed blessing. To face extreme limitations and to be aware of that can be more of a burden than some people can bear.

That sounds somewhat heartless, I know, but it turns out that those doctors were not far off the mark. Wanda told me that Henie often talked to her about how tired she was of her body — how she wished she could walk and keep up with others, how she could talk and be immediately and generally understood, how she could eat tacos and not leave half the meat on her chest and lap. Her main hope was for a new body in heaven. She loved verses about rising up on wings of eagles and running and not being weary. Wonderful verses, to be sure, but Henie's attraction to them would occasionally grow very dangerous, like the time she was riding with Wanda and suddenly took off her seatbelt, unlocked and pushed the door open as far as she could manage, and started to lean out as if to let herself fall onto the pavement. Wanda managed to grab her and pull her back before she got too much of her weight off the car seat.

Having to live with the constant and keen knowledge of her limitations perhaps also helps explain why Henie, after she left high school and could find no productive work to do, became intensely anxious so often. She hated change; for her everything had to stay the same, be familiar, be predictable. Her parents had decided that they simply could not face the possibility of putting her into an institution, so they kept her at home, where she, sometimes with the aid of drugs, slept through most days and watched television movies through most nights. Change her routine a little, and she would be thrown off. As I mentioned, she would visit our house, but if one of our sons had a friend over when Henie came to visit, Henie almost immediately moved from some level of apparent comfort to some stage of fear. And then the symptoms of anxiety, as Wanda had catalogued them for me, would start to make their ugliness known.

When she was comfortable, though, she showed some remarkable abilities. She seemed uncannily skilled in reading social situations and what was on people's minds. She especially seemed able to tell when Wanda, I, or one of our sons had something bothering us. "What's wrong?" she would ask through Wanda, and I would have to admit that I couldn't quite decide how to respond to a student who had been missing one of my classes frequently. If I told her about such cases, and voiced my suspicions that the student was choosing just to sleep in, Henie would invariably let me know about other possible interpretations — about absences due to headaches or mono or cramps, for example. Often it would turn out that Henie was right. She was always on the side of those she thought were suffering.

Wanda also frequently talked about Henie's marked ability for prayer. When Henie was Wanda's student, they often started school days with prayer, and Wanda said she was always amazed at how Henie knew what or who in the life of the school needed prayer and at how Henie expressed herself to God. Her prayers, in fact, seemed parts of much longer, intimate conversations with God, parts that she was letting Wanda and sometimes others overhear. She talked to God as if she were talking to a loved one tucking her into bed at night.

When I had told Wanda that maybe I could help her with Henie through some of the hours of Henie's brother's wedding and reception, I had in mind some adjustments to my plans for the day. I had previously set that day aside for musky hunting on Murray Lake, and I still intended to devote most of that day to slinging lures. But why not use a couple of hours of the long day to take Wanda and Henie along in the boat? We could tour parts of the lake (Wanda loved looking at cottages from their lake side), and maybe I could show Henie a little about musky fishing.

Wanda loved my suggestion. If they were to drive out and hop in the boat with me just after suppertime or so, they could enjoy some time outside and break up the long span between two and whenever Henie's folks got back from the reception.

I was on the lake already in the early afternoon, and by the time I met Wanda and Henie at the west launch, I had had some musky follows, but I hadn't yet enticed a fish to eat. So taking a little break from fishing didn't seem like some form of folly or sacrifice.

Hop was definitely the wrong word to use to describe how Henie got into my boat. I tied the boat up both fore and aft securely to the dock. Then Wanda moved close to Henie on the dock, wrapped her arms around her waist, and urged her to step toward me in the boat. I took Henie's arms, and I have to admit that I thought they would be rather limp and weak. But they were stiff and taut, like small cables drawn almost to the breaking point. She led with an uncertain leg toward me, and once she came down toward the boat and Wanda released her, I would have fallen over backwards with her in my arms had I not propped a foot against the base of my fishing seat. I didn't fall, but Henie had most of her body leaning heavily against me before I could help her toward a seat in the back. "Sawy, sawy, sawy," Henie repeated, almost ready to cry, and I gathered that she was embarrassed by so much clumsy physical contact. Some people would probably have blamed me, but in Henie's case, whenever something turned out to be wrong or awkward around her, she invariably assumed it was her fault.

As Wanda then stepped down into the boat and took a seat next to Henie, I started putting a life jacket on and handed one to each of them. "Time for life jackets," I said; "we don't want the Coast Guard to be unhappy with us, do we?" The fact is that no member of the Coast Guard was within thirty miles of Murray Lake; it's just that if Henie had thought about throwing herself out of a car, it might occur to her that an easier way to go would involve leaning back over the gunnel and flipping into the lake.

I started a counterclockwise tour of the lake, doing little more than idling along, staying thirty or forty yards off the dock heads. Wanda was intrigued by the contrasts in lakeside structures; some houses had to be worth a half million dollars or more, and many of them looked even more expensive than what they probably were since they stood next to little two-bedroom cottages that were not even as big as the garages attached to the fancy houses. Henie was much more interested in the geese swimming around and sunning on the shore. Most geese couples had had goslings in the past week or so, and the goslings on the water clearly had only one thing on their minds — making sure that their mother never got more than a yard or two away from them.

"Yeah," I broke into Wanda's and Henie's looking, albeit in

different directions, "I've heard that there's been a lot of te-
ment out here lately with all the newly hatched geese."

"What do you mean?" Wanda clearly had no clue wha
talking about.

"Well, muskies will eat just about anything — d
muskrats, little dogs that fall off the dock. Anglers postin
the Michigan Muskie Alliance board have been writing ab
how they've been casting in one direction when they hear t
huge commotion in the water and turn to see a honking a
hissing mother goose circling around goose down floating
the water — "

"Not now." Wanda gave me a stern look. "It's you again and
TMI; we don't need all those details. Why don't you show us
how you fish for muskies."

"Okay, good idea. Let me motor over that way fifty yards or
so. The boys and I call this stretch the Dinner Table because
we've had so much action here the past few years. We set the
table and the muskies come to dine. So here, Henie, is the kind
of bait we often use. This is an in-line spinner with double-ten
blades. Careful — don't touch the hooks. They're so sharp they
can make you bleed. Watch — I'll cast it out just a little and
you can see the blades spin and the skirt puff out and pulse.
See? Good. I'm not sure what in the real world it's supposed to
look like, but it catches fish. Maybe it's something about the vi-
brations the blades give off that drives the fish wild. Okay, now
I'll give it a good long cast, and as I get it close to the boat,
look really closely behind and below it to see if a musky is following. It'll look like a big greenish-brown torpedo. If I get a
follow, I'll do a quick turn at the boat and try to get it to hit —
sometimes they hit just when they think the bait is getting

See, here the spinner comes. See any follow? Is there a big
behind it?"

"Ooooh," Henie exclaimed, drooling a little, "wah dat?" And
pointed.

"Huh?" I had no idea what she was asking about.

Wanda knew: "What are all those minnows doing? They
come flying out of the water in a big arc ahead of your lure,
hit the surface, and then skip into the air again. That's what
Henie sees. They look like a bunch of silvery darts. What are
they doing?"

"Ah, okay. Those minnows see the flash of my lure and think
it's a big fish out to gobble them up. I think they must be little
shiners. Flying out of the water like that is a classic avoidance
maneuver. But you and Henie have to watch behind my lure,
not in front of it. If a musky appears, it'll be behind the lure,
maybe a few feet behind it. You really gotta pay attention or
you'll miss the musky. Here goes another cast."

Maybe it was some small miracle, but that cast did call up a
musky out of the weeds within a few feet of having landed.
"Look," I hissed, "look now, right over there, about a foot behind my lure. It's a musky, a pretty big musky. See its back? See
the wake it's leaving? And in front of my lure the shiners are going crazy — they're really jumping and scattering now. Here it
comes. I'm gonna speed my lure up. Quiet, quiet, quiet, and
don't move — maybe I can get this baby to hit."

I did a smooth L-turn at the side of the boat, but the fish saw
something — maybe one of us flinched a little — and turned
sharply away from my bucktail and vanished back into the dark.

"Shoot, shoot, shoot — I thought I was gonna hook that
one. That would have been great — a boatside hookset on a

pretty big fish. That baby was about forty-three, forty-four inches long. You guys would've been able to net it, right? I think we would have all gotten wet with the splashing. Maybe I can call up another fish and get it to eat."

"That's all right," Wanda said, "that was very cool. I didn't really expect to see a follow since sometimes you and the boys go out all day long and have only a couple among all of you. And I didn't expect to see a fish come so close to biting. I'm glad we came out with you. We got to see some impressive cottages, lots of big and little geese, and one mean-looking musky. We'll have to come out with you again some night. But now I think we should head back to town. Which way is the dock? I'm kinda turned around out here."

After I dropped Wanda and Henie off at the dock and watched them get in the car and drive away, I stayed on the lake for a few more hours, and I had three more follows, but those fish weren't even as aggressive as the one that had appeared to all three of us.

Once I got back home and had unpacked my gear, just a little before midnight, Wanda found me making notes about my trip in my office, wrapped her arms around my neck, and gave me a long kiss on the top of my head.

"I know I'm pretty lovable, but what's that for?" I asked.

"Special thanks."

"Yeah? For what?"

"For coming up with the idea of having us drive out to the lake and for giving us that tour and demonstration."

"It wasn't that big of a deal."

"Well, to us it was. For me it really broke up almost nine hours of watching Henie. And that time in the boat really made an impression on her. She even prayed about it."

"She did? What's up with that?"

"Well, her folks always call about twenty minutes before they pick her up, and that's the time we usually have a little prayer together before she tells me how much she loves me and says goodbye."

"If she's gonna pray about being in the boat, she should've prayed that all the muskies that follow my lure in the future would actually bite," I joked. "Now there's a prayer that would make sense."

"Maybe to you, but not to Henie."

"I don't get it. What in the world did she pray for, then?"

"For those minnows. All those little fish flying out of the water in front of your lure."

"You got to be kidding me. She prayed for a bunch of little shiners? Most of them don't have half a chance anyway. Some will have a fin or their tail bitten off. Some will be eaten whole. Some will catch some kind of disease and rot to death."

"Somehow she must have known all that."

"And what makes you say so?"

"She said it in her prayer. She said, 'Lord, please help those minnows skip away and have a chance to grow up.'"

From Russia with Love

Ever since she learned it was a possibility for her, my sister, Barb, made it clear that she wanted to be a mother. No matter that she grew up in a time when some of feminism's loudest and most strident voices were proclaiming that to become pregnant was to sacrifice control of one's body and become subject to the hegemony of men. No matter at all. She wanted — in fact, she felt called — to give birth, probably more than once.

As we all learn fairly early in our lives, the most common and socially accepted way to become a mother is to find, love, and marry a man. I have to admit that I do not know many of the details of my sister's early romantic history, mainly because as she — nine years younger than I — moved into her high-school years, I left the family home and moved to Chicago for graduate school and several years of high school teaching. And even if I had stayed at or near home, I'm not sure how much she would have told me. So what little I learned about whom she dated and for how long came at second or third hand.

I do know for certain that after I moved back to Grand Rapids with Wanda, my new bride, Barb had a terrible breakup. She had dated Jim for so long that no one could remember exactly when the relationship had started. His personality — apparently confident and carefree — went well with hers. Everyone in our extended family liked Jim, and everyone in Jim's extended family liked Barb. Plus Barb and Jim had more interests in common than two people could ordinarily expect to have.

So what caused the breakup? You've heard of it, I'm sure: MFCD, or Male Fear of Commitment Disorder. The breakup, it seemed, was really a long series of calling things off, then getting back together, then calling things off again, until finally it was absurd to try to patch things up yet again. The whole business left Barb hurt, confused, and desolate. Everyone in our extended family had been praying for Barb to find the right someone, but for all the answers possible for God to give us, it seemed that he had settled on "not yet."

"Not yet" feels a lot like "no," but it's not truly absolute. And after a while I started hearing from my mom and dad that Barb's coworkers were trying to set her up with a supervisor from an adjacent office, Brian. He had apparently always made it known that he wouldn't date a fellow employee, but Barb's friends kept all sorts of not-very-subtle pressure on him, and eventually he gave in and asked Barb out. All the pressure turned out to be worth it because after a respectably long time of dating (according to my mom), Barb and Brian married.

The fact that Barb and Brian were both around forty years old at the time perhaps should have given us some hint, but really, how were we relatives supposed to deal with the fact that the two of them had trouble conceiving?

"Maybe they're not really trying," family friends would whisper.

"Oh no," my mom or dad would respond, "they're trying all right."

I never learned how my parents knew that. Nor did I ever learn what wasn't working with Barb and Brian. I did learn that the worst day for Barb in each one of all those years of frustration, the day when she could never bring herself to go to church, was Mother's Day. And ultimately I came to believe that in response to the family's prayers for a child for Barb and Brian, God's answer was "no."

But I clearly didn't know everything I needed to know about how God works, since Barb and Brian had some friends who referred them to other people who knew yet some other people who had had wonderful experiences with something no one in our extended family had ever given a thought to, except in connection with other families — adoption.

So after a seemingly endless period of exploration and negotiation, Barb and Brian left for Irkutsk, Russia, and then returned a few weeks later with two sons. They had always wanted two children, they said, so why not adopt two at the same time from the same place? One boy, Misha, they renamed Zach, and the other, Alexei, they renamed Scott. Zach was a year and a half old at the time, and Scott was ten months. They were both so tiny that I thought I could hold one in my left hand, one in my right, and not have to worry about dropping either.

But they grew and flourished — they crawled, they took faltering steps and then plopped backwards, they walked, they started poking into everything — especially all things mechanical — around their house, and they loved climbing and hanging on their cousins on our side of the family. These eight cousins were then in their late teens or early twenties. Some of them were married. And so their most natural concerns and forms of recreation were not identical to Zach's and Scott's.

What was particularly fascinating to me was that Barb wanted her boys to have the same experiences as those eight cousins had had when they were young. She seemed almost obsessive about this. I didn't fully understand it, but I didn't dare interfere.

So Barb and Brian took up camping, first in a tent, then in a pop-up trailer, and finally in a close-to-luxurious house trailer. And they camped where my brothers and I and our wives had camped with our kids. When our kids were really young, we usually camped at some state park along the Lake Michigan shoreline, often at Grand Haven's notorious Diaper Alley. Little kids, no matter what they did, couldn't get too dirty in beach sand. When the cousins were older and could hike along at a respectable pace on their own, we camped at our extended family's all-time favorite state park, Ludington. Barb, Brian, Zach, and Scott followed in our footsteps, just several years after us.

When her boys were just starting school (preschool and kindergarten), Barb decided it was time to take them to the Station. The full name of the Station is the University of Michigan Biological Station, in Pellston, Michigan, about four hours north of Grand Rapids. This is where my brother Bob is the resident biologist, and on the grounds of the Station he and Meredy, his wife, reared their two daughters.

Members of my extended family have stayed in rooms in the dorm at the Station in all seasons over the course of many years. During those seasons, we've enjoyed all sorts of activities —

scavenging apples and making cider; skating and ice fishing and playing dangerously fierce games of broomball on the ice; collecting sap and distilling an embarrassingly small amount of maple syrup; and hiking, biking, and swimming. When Barb started asking as many of us in the extended family as possible to accompany her family on a fall trip to the Station, I was elated. Not because the trip would allow me to scrounge around abandoned homesteads near the Station for fallen apples that were good for nothing other than cider. But because I saw the Station as perhaps the best place on earth to introduce Zach and Scott to something I believed they simply had to know about if they were to become full-fledged members of our extended family — fishing.

The main building at the Station, rising three stories above the shores of Douglas Lake, is called the Lakeside Lab. Perhaps the most striking feature of the Lab is its boatwell; its builders dug a channel from the lake into the bottom floor of the Lab so that researchers at the Station could steer pontoon boats from the lake directly into the Lab and tie them up there. I never saw the Lab primarily as a haven for moored boats. I saw it as the only building I knew of that had been built around a fishing hole.

People can sit on the concrete edge of the boatwell, or set up lawn chairs along that edge, and always be protected from wind, rain, snow, or sleet. Since there are lights in the Lab, people can fish there at any time of day or night. And since station administrators do not want the boatwell to freeze, they keep the lower level of the Lab at a constant moderate temperature during the fall and winter. Best of all, over the years of fishing the boatwell, I had learned that a school of big rock bass hides out there and that these fish become especially aggressive biters in the fall. So wouldn't you agree that a fall trip to the Station would provide me with the practically perfect chance to teach my two young nephews to fish?

Of the twenty-four people in our extended family, only seventeen were able to make the trip to the Station. But that number was close enough to the number that prevailed for most of our earlier trips that Barb was satisfied.

I prepared for the trip by rigging up the rods that our sons Jon, Joel, and Jason had used when I was teaching them how to fish — one rod for Zach, one for Scott, and one for me in case I was ever not too busy with my nephews to use it. And I bought enough nightcrawlers and waxworms so that we could keep the rock bass in the boatwell occupied for a good long time.

When we all got to the station late on a Friday night, I found that I was going to have to work within some pretty severe restrictions that Barb had put in place. Earlier she had learned from Bob that the man who in the past had pressed our apples into cider had retired and dismantled his press. But she had also learned that researchers at the Station had discovered the remains of a significant Native settlement on the north shore of Burt Lake, within reasonable hiking distance of the Station, and she had decided that such a hike and exploration were just too good of an educational opportunity for her sons to miss.

So there went most of our Saturday morning at the Station and my dream of using all or most of that day to teach Zach and Scott more than a smidgeon of what I knew about catch-and-release rock bass. But I will still have most of the afternoon, I thought. I held that thought until lunchtime, when my youngest brother, Bruce, invited everyone to set off model rockets, an offer that left my two young nephews practically bouncing with eagerness to sprint up to the ball field, the area that Bob had designated as the only safe rocket-launch site.

As it turned out, then, it wasn't until late on Saturday afternoon that Barb released the boys into my care and instruction. I gave them some gear to carry to the Lab, I grabbed the rest, and then I ran one last mental inventory to make sure I hadn't forgotten anything. Just before we set out, Barb called the boys to her side. She was whispering to them intently. All I was able to make out was something about being careful and something about supper. Nothing about paying close attention to their Uncle Bill. "Just so you know, now they're going to experience something they'll never forget," I called over to her.

It took us only about ten minutes to walk from the dorm to the Lab. And it didn't take me even that long to get their rods rigged up with a bobber, a sinker, a hook and a piece of nightcrawler. And then we got bait in the water, Scott next to me near the big sliding door, Zach closer to one of the moored pontoons.

For a while, not much happened. Either Zach's or Scott's bobber would wobble a bit now and then, but when the young angler would snap the rod as I had shown them in my "here's-how-you-set-the-hook" talk, all he ever pulled out of the water was a bare hook.

Then the fears that had assaulted me years earlier with my sons returned, as intense as they had ever been: *This can't go on, I worried, or I'm gonna lose them as fishermen. It's time to try something else. We need fish on the line.*

So I set both of them up to fish somewhat deeper. And we three moved onto the deck of the pontoon moored as far back in the boatwell as it was possible to go; there I had the boys start exploring the dark water behind and alongside the boat.

Then we got into some fish. Rock bass for sure, but also some bluegills, several sunfish, and a few feisty little smallmouth bass. It seemed as if I had been drawn twenty years backwards in a hole in time and was trying to keep up with Jon, Joel, and Jason. We had fish thrashing around on the surface, fish slapping against the boat's pontoons or flipping off hooks swung up over the pontoon's deck, lines and attached bobbers being whipped around my head, and Zach using his thumbnail to slice nightcrawlers into chunks and then volley them across the deck to Scott.

I loved it.

But then Scott drew my attention away from the fishing: "Uncle Bill, what time is it? Mom said we had to be back at the dorm by suppertime. And that's at 6:30. Is it close to 6:30 yet? She wants to make sure that everyone has supper together."

I almost choked. "Go back? Are you serious? We're fishing right now, and we're into fish big time. Who knows when we'll ever find fish as hungry as these again? It's almost 6:30, but your mom and the others will hold supper back for us or save some food in the oven. We won't go hungry. Here, let me get a fresh chunk of crawler on your hook."

"Not now. We have to be on time. Mom said it's really important. Plus she told us we have to be careful with what you tell us, anyway."

"She said that? She must have been joking. I hardly ever mess around with what I tell you guys. Maybe with her. And with your dad now and then. But not with you guys."

Zach took over for Scott: "That's what our mom said. And she meant it. I could tell. C'mon, Scott, we'd better start back to the dorm."

"All right — I give in. Time to pack everything up. I guess we'll have to try to educate the rest of these fish some other time."

When we got back to the dorm, Barb was sitting near the door.

"Okay, little sister, we're back in time. But I have to say that I'm not really sure about these two boys of yours. It took us a little while, but eventually we got into some fish. I mean, Zach and Scott were doing some big-time catching. And then out of the blue they tell me that you said they had to be back by 6:30 for supper. Leaving a bunch of fish that are biting — who ever heard of such craziness? It was about as clear as anything that these two are missing the Vande Kopple fishing gene. How are we ever going to get them to be true members of this family if they put stuff like dinner before fishing?"

"Maybe they'll grow up and have their priorities straight."

"Hunh — not very likely."

Just then Aunt Judy announced that supper was ready. And we did what we had often done in the past — spread ourselves out along both sides of a long table and dug in to an excellent spaghetti and lasagna supper. There we sat, muscles soothed by the heat of the wood stove, seeing nothing out on the lake except for one security light punctuating the coast of North Fishtail Bay, hearing absolutely no traffic or sirens or planes.

And then we started to retell the stories about family times at the Station. I got a good one in about the time my dad returned there after a trip to Cheboygan for minnows, opened the door of our shanty to add his bait to the minnow bucket, saw the heavy northern pike I had caught in his absence and then left on a stringer in the shanty hole, and — apparently acting on some primitive instinct — grabbed a spear and ran the defenseless pike through.

Dad got back at me by telling about the time he — right where we were sitting — opened my Christmas present to him of a hair dryer and could find absolutely no way to disguise the fact that it, in all its rose-colored glory, was probably the very last thing on earth he needed or wanted.

The stories flowed one into another — Zach and Scott butting in whenever they found a tiny opening to get their own jokes and wisecracks in — until it was time to clear the table and get everything cleaned up before bed.

About two weeks after our trip to the Station, I received a very short e-mail message from Barb. All she had written was, "See attached." What was attached was a scan of a very rough drawing, a drawing with almost twenty stick figures, long and short, sitting around a table next to a huge contraption. I have very little patience for trying to figure out such mysteries via e-mail, so I called Barb at work:

"Okay, I give up. What is it?"

"What?"

"You know what — the stick-figure sketch you sent me as an attachment."

"Oh, that. Can't you figure out what it is?"

"If I could, would I be calling you?"

"Okay, well, it's a picture of all of us during story time after Saturday supper up at the dorm."

"It is?"

"Sure. Don't you see the wood stove off to the side?"

"You mean that thing that looks like an antique steam locomotive without the wheels?"

"Yep."

"So where did the drawing come from?"

"For school Zach had to draw a picture of what his teacher called a 'super-happy time in his life,' and he decided to draw a picture of our Saturday evening meal up north. Scott helped him."

"That's his happy time? I would have thought his happy time was down at the boatwell. Anyway, what's with all the strange clusters of letters?"

"The boys tried to label people. Zach's teacher is encouraging him to try invented spelling, so what you see are his best attempts at spelling people's names. Scott added a suggestion or two."

"Did they try to label me?"

"Sure. Don't you see it?"

"Can't say that I do."

"Do you see the long figure toward the back on the right? The one with his arms in the air?"

"That's me?"

"Yep."

"How do you know that?"

"Look just to the left of your head. See?"

"I see two clusters of letters, but they're awfully small. Hold on — I'll try it with my reading glasses. Okay, it says 'Onkl Bull.'

Yeah, it says 'Onkl Bull.' That's what the boys put down for me?"

"Yep." She couldn't cover her laughter.

"Very funny. Very, very funny."

"What? 'Onkl Bull' for 'Uncle Bill.' Not bad for little guys just learning their letters. And somehow it fits, don't you think?"

Mother Might Know Best

"So, Uncle Bill, is this a really good way for me to catch pike? Will it be better than tolling?"

"You mean trolling?"

"Yeah, I guess — trolling. Will this be better? I didn't do so good with that."

"For sure, Scott. When I get us all set up, I've got a story to tell you about how great this kind of fishing can be."

Scott, one of my adopted-from-Russia nephews, and I were anchored just off what my sons call "Jackpot Point," the prominent point on the south side of the entrance to Duck Bay in the Les Cheneaux Islands area. Earlier in the day I had taken him and his brother, Zach, out trolling for pike, and Zach had caught three more pike than Scott had. So now, just before supper, hoping to even the score with his slightly older brother, Scott had begged me to take him and him alone out for another chance at some pike. Since earlier he had had some trouble telling when his trolled lure was fouled with weeds, I decided to anchor off Jackpot Point and get him set up to still fish with some chubs as bait. Hook them through the lips so that they can swim around naturally, wait for the pike to find them, let the line run free until the pike take the chubs well into their mouths, and then set the hook.

As we had loaded our gear in the boat, Barb, my sister and Scott's mother, walked over from the beach and had some strict words for us: "I guess it's okay if you go out for a bit, but tonight, you should remember, is the night when we're all going out for supper. We've got reservations at that waterfront place in Cedarville, and we leave in one hour. One hour exactly. You've got to be back then. I don't care how fast the fish are biting or how many bald eagles you're seeing or what jokes you're in the middle of telling or anything else — you've got to be back here in time. And Scotty, you're going to have to take my watch and be the responsible one. You know that if Uncle Bill gets interested in what's going on out there, he'll forget about everything back on shore and want to stay out there forever. So you'll have to watch the time and stay after him. Can you do that, Scotty? Can you make sure you two are back at the dock in time? You can't let him talk you into staying out past our time to leave for the restaurant."

"Sure, Mom, you know I can. I'll keep a close eye on the time."

I pretended to be offended: "Not exactly sure how you've developed that view of me, little sister. I can't think of a bit of evidence that I lack proper discipline."

"Oh, sure. You know that if the fish get active you're going to get that focus you get — one thing and one thing only on your mind. You always do. Plus you were pretty strict when your own three sons were growing up, but now when you're with our boys, whatever wild and crazy stuff they want to do, you not only let them — you egg them on. Or suggest stuff for them. No point in trying to argue — you know I'm right. After Zach and Scott spend time with you, it takes Brian and me almost two days to get them settled down and back on the right track."

"Just having a little fun. Not enough fun in the world."

"You both heard me. And Scott, you remember what I said. Now you better get going or you won't have any time at all."

"So do you want to hear that story about how fantastic this kind of fishing can be?" I had gotten the legal number of rods rigged up for Scott and me. Hooked chubs were swimming around to the east of the point, right off the tip of the point, and to the west of the point. With the number and spread of our bait, even though our time was limited, I was fairly confident that we'd have some action and that Scott might get his number of pike up to Zach's.

"Okay, Uncle Bill, tell me that story." Scott had piled up a couple of boat cushions in the bow and was sitting high up on them, periodically switching his gaze from one of our lines to the next and then the next.

"Okay, the story comes from Mark, the owner of the resort we're staying at this week. Have you seen him at all?"

"The guy who goes around and scoops up the goose poop?"

"Yeah, that's him. He's got to figure out some way to keep the geese off the lawn; that plastic fox isn't working. Anyway, this past spring, on the first day of pike season for the U.P., he took his boat out to this point, right where we are. He beached the boat on the shore, probably just over there, and then threw out some chubs just like we're doing, one on that side of the point over there, and one just behind us there. Then he pulled a folding chair from his boat, sat down on the beach, and waited."

"Uncle Bill, look at this line — it's moving a little. Is it a pike?"

I took the rod and held the line gently between my thumb and forefinger. "Naw, Scott, that's no pike yet. Line's moving too slowly. And I can feel the little twitches. It's just a pretty active minnow. It'll probably settle down as it gets more tired." I leaned the rod back against the gunnel. "Where was I? Yeah, so Mark got some chubs in the water. After only about fifteen minutes, the line went peeling fast off one of his reels, the one, I guess, that was nearest his boat. The line went out like crazy, and then stopped. Then it started going out again. So he was almost positive he had a pike on. He counted to two hundred and then set the hook as hard as he could. He told me it was like setting a hook into a stump — just really solid with no give. He started to wonder whether he actually had a fish on or not; he was there holding on to his bent pole, and the line was going into the water and just staying there. It almost seemed like a big snag. But then you know what?"

"What?"

"His line started to move."

"It did? Has that ever happened to you?"

"Yeah, once or twice, but always only on really big fish. I mean really big. It was weird, Mark said, because the fish didn't jump or thrash or shake its head or anything like that; it just started to swim very calmly out away from shore, smooth and steady like."

"Did it get away?"

"Nope. Mark started putting as much pressure on it as he dared. He said he could feel that the line was close to the breaking point. He adjusted his drag until he thought it was set perfectly. He would pull some more, then ease off when the fish was taking drag constantly, then pull some more. And little by little by little, he was able to ease that fish back toward him. At that point he was sure it was a monster. In fact, he told me, he wondered whether he had hooked some sixty-pound catfish or something, but he had never heard of a catfish being caught up around here, so he figured he maybe had a record pike on his line. But he hadn't gotten a single glimpse of it."

"So he was just standing there holding on and watching his line move through the water?"

"Yeah, and for a fisherman that's a really tense time. So much inside tells you to get impatient and pull harder. But he knew what he was doing and played that fish until each time he pulled on it he could bring it toward him a little bit more. When he got it into water shallow enough that he could see most of its back, he told me, he almost hyperventilated."

"What's that?"

"He was breathing way too fast. Because you know how big that fish was? A fish that was fooled by a chub on a little hook? You have any idea?"

"Thirty inches?"

"Thirty inches? You kidding me? Thirty inches is nothing to sneeze at, true, but we're talking about a real monster here. This beast, Mark figured out, had to be at least four feet long. Four feet! That's almost as long as you are, right?"

"Almost. I'm nine years old and already four foot three. That's pretty tall, don't you think?"

"Yeah. So if you jumped in the water and started swimming around, you'd be about the size of that pike. Anyway, Mark stayed patient and kept easing the monster toward him. Every once in a while, of course, the fish would realize how shallow the water was that it was getting into and turn and make another run out toward the deep. And then Mark would go through the whole process again. He had to figure that each time the fish made a run and then got eased back toward the shallows it would get a little more tired. Finally, he managed to pull it up onto the mud in front of his feet, where the fish just sat, its gills working like mad. Then something pretty surprising happened."

"What? An eagle swooped down and tried to steal it?"

"No way. An eagle could never lift a fish that size. What happened was that some people who were staying at Mark's resort happened to come trolling by, and when they got an idea about how big that fish was, they decided they should run their boat up on shore and send their son over to help Mark get that fish entirely out of the water. The thing was, this kid was huge — he was tall and broad. He must have weighed three hundred pounds. And he was more than a little clumsy. So he jumped out of his folks' beached boat, lumbered over toward Mark, and just as he was getting close, he stumbled and fell headfirst right into the shallow water, just a few feet from the fish."

"Serious?"

"No lie. He stumbled into the water right by the pike, and you can guess what all that noise and commotion did. That fish, as tired as it was, went into a panic. It started thrashing around in that shallow water, shaking its head, whipping its tail around, flipping over on itself a couple of times. And in one of those flips, it threw the hook, sat there a bit, almost stunned, and then swam away slowly until it was resting right under the rear of Mark's boat."

"It got away?"

"Hold on a second. Don't get ahead of me. So Mark was standing there almost in shock because the fish of his lifetime just came unhooked, the kid was on his hands and knees in the water all muddied up because of the fish's thrashing and the kid's fall, and the fish was about five yards away resting below Mark's boat. And then — you just can't believe stuff like this — the kid apparently felt so bad about messing things up that he did something crazy. This was one of those times when they say 'don't try this at home.' The kid glanced at Mark, saw that the fish was still not swimming away, and then he dove headfirst into the water and went for the fish. It's true. It was the middle of May in the Upper Peninsula, so that water had to be about forty-five degrees. Not much warmer than that. Cold enough to stop lots of hearts. But that kid dove in, swam over, grabbed the pike, kicked his way back to where he could stand up, got his feet under him, and then stood up, using both hands to hold that pike against his chest."

"Uncle Bill . . ."

"I just checked the lines, Scott — no takers yet."

"But . . ."

"I'm serious — I just checked the lines and no pike is running away with any of them. So the kid was standing there soaking wet and shivering like mad, but he had the pike tight to his chest. He must have felt as if he had redeemed himself, and then — I wouldn't believe this myself if I didn't know Mark pretty well — that pike found some last bit of strength, flexed its body, shook itself violently, and fell back into the water. By that time, if I had been Mark, I'm not sure what I would have done to that kid."

"Uncle Bill . . ."

"Just a second, Scott, I'm coming to the really good part."

"But . . ."

"I'll get there. You got to remember that the water where those guys were was all muddied up with the thrashing and walking and swimming and all. So they couldn't see where that pike was. So what do you think they did?"

"I don't know, and . . ."

"This is the best part of all. What they did was, well, they both dropped down on their knees and started to feel around like a couple of blind guys in hopes that they would find that pike. There they were — crawling and reaching and feeling all over in that soup. Can you imagine how desperate you'd be to try to find that fish? And after a couple of minutes — "

"Uncle Bill, hold on a second! We've got to get going. You keep talking, and now we've only got five minutes to get back to the dock. I've been checking the watch. I promised my mom we'd be back in time. I don't want to make her mad. We have to head back."

"But don't you want to hear the end of the story? Just because we've got reservations at some restaurant doesn't mean we should leave the water right toward the end of a great story. What's a meal compared to a story? Everybody gets a bunch of meals in their lives but not so many stories."

"Please, we've got to go. We've got to go now." He had a lot of moisture in his eyes and desperation in his tone.

"All right. All right. I'll pack stuff up and roar back to the dock. Guess we did need a little more time to catch something ourselves. No way I want to be some big black sheep in the family. But I'm going to have to talk to your mother about priorities."

As we bounced our way full throttle through the chop of Snows Channel to our dock, Scott sat in the bow. Sure enough — Barb was standing on the outermost dock gazing in our direction. The closer we got, the more manically Scott waved.

When we glided into our slip about fifteen yards inside of the outer dock, Scott stood up, wrapped a rope loosely around a cedar post, and called to his fast-approaching mother: "I tried, Mom, I really tried. But Uncle Bill was started on a story and hardly let me talk. Are we really late? Am I in trouble? I tried the best I could, I really did."

"It's okay, Scotty. You guys are only a minute or two late, and the restaurant shouldn't be too upset if we're just a tad tardy. I'm glad you showed some responsibility. Uncle Bill was telling you a story, huh?"

"Yeah, Mom, it was this crazy story about a giant fish and a giant kid, and Uncle Bill didn't get to finish it because I finally got him to start back this way. Do you think he can finish it when we're all together at supper?"

"Probably. We'll have time. And maybe it won't be too noisy. He can start over so we all know what's going on. And then he can finish it. But on the way there, I've got to tell you a thing or two. There's some stuff about your uncle's stories that you need to know."